Readers Love ANDREW GREY

Paint by Number

"This story, like most of Andrew's books is sweet and full of feelings… If you've never read a book from Andrew Grey and even if you have, I highly recommend this one."

—Open Skye Book Reviews

"There is a saying that you can never go home again but this story will prove an exception to that."

—Paranormal Romance Guild

Hard Road Back

"I urge you to grab a copy of Hard Road Back so you too can discover and enjoy Martin and Scarborough's world."

—Love Bytes

Catch of a Lifetime

"…a salute to Mr. Grey's mastery of gay locution, which added enormously to my reading pleasure."

—Rainbow Book Reviews

Twice Baked

"This a great second chance romance novel… There is loads of charm and romance."

—MM Good Book Reviews

"A fun and flirty story I enjoyed and I believe you will, too."

—Bayou Book Junkie

By Andrew Grey

Published by DREAMSPINNER PRESS
www.dreamspinnerpress.com

By ANDREW GREY (cont'd)

Published by DREAMSPINNER PRESS
www.dreamspinnerpress.com

By ANDREW GREY (cont'd)

STORIES FROM THE RANGE
A Shared Range
A Troubled Range
An Unsettled Range
A Foreign Range
An Isolated Range
A Volatile Range
A Chaotic Range

STRANDED
Stranded
Taken

TALES FROM KANSAS
Dumped in Oz
Stuck in Oz
Trapped in Oz

TALES FROM ST. GILES
Taming the Beast
Redeeming the Stepbrother

TASTE OF LOVE
A Taste of Love
A Serving of Love
A Helping of Love
A Slice of Love

WITHOUT BORDERS
A Heart Without Borders
A Spirit Without Borders

WORK OUT
Spot Me
Pump Me Up
Core Training
Crunch Time
Positive Resistance
Personal Training
Cardio Conditioning
Work Me Out Anthology

Published by DREAMSPINNER PRESS
www.dreamspinnerpress.com

FIRE AND GLASS

ANDREW GREY

Published by
DREAMSPINNER PRESS

5032 Capital Circle SW, Suite 2, PMB# 279, Tallahassee, FL 32305-7886 USA
www.dreamspinnerpress.com

This is a work of fiction. Names, characters, places, and incidents either are the product of author imagination or are used fictitiously, and any resemblance to actual persons, living or dead, business establishments, events, or locales is entirely coincidental.

Fire and Glass
© 2022 Andrew Grey

Cover Art
© 2022 L.C. Chase
http://www.lcchase.com
Cover content is for illustrative purposes only and any person depicted on the cover is a model.

Mass Market Paperback ISBN: 978-1-64108-372-0
Trade Paperback ISBN: 978-1-64108-371-3
Digital ISBN: 978-1-64108-370-6
Digital eBook published November 2022
v. 1.0

Printed in the United States of America

For Dominic, who is always there for me, no matter what.

CHAPTER 1

STATE TROOPER Casey Bombaro grumbled as he sat in his patrol car at the start of the workday, the summer sun beating in the windows, and read his messages. He already had two break-in reports to investigate, and he needed to get them looked into. Now he had a message to come in to the office outside Carlisle to pick something up.

At least one of the reported break-ins was between his current location and town, so it wouldn't be a wasted trip. He responded to the message and quickly scanned the others before buckling up.

One of the things he loved about being a state trooper was that his car was his office. He didn't sit at a desk in some building pushing paper all day. He was out in the trenches, the primary law-enforcement presence for a good part of his district, and Casey liked it when the area under his patrol was quiet. It hadn't been for the past few months. Casey thought something had changed—the robberies were becoming more frequent, and those responsible were getting bolder—but he wasn't making progress getting to the source, which frustrated him no end.

After starting the engine, he pulled out of his driveway and used GPS to guide him to the address of the break-in. It was typical of what he'd been finding—the owners came home from a night out to find their home had been broken into. Easily sold electronics were gone, and so was the liquor. Medicine cabinet stripped of prescription meds, and any available jewelry cases or boxes were missing. Nothing else was touched, and no messes were made. In each case, the thieves seemed to know what they were looking for and got in and out, leaving very little trace of themselves. The fuckers knew what they were doing, and that ground at Casey. The jobs were small-time enough, no big score up to this point, and yet the break-ins kept happening, sometimes three or four a week.

He made notes about the incident, but unfortunately he could offer little hope of recovery. He added the report to his list of things to do and headed to the station.

"We got a big job for you," Collins, the sergeant in charge, said with an evil smile as he handed Casey a cup of coffee. Then he set a small, battered beige fabric purse on his desk. "This was found behind a business in Newville. It was turned over to the township, and they passed it on to us to try to return. There was ID inside, so sometime today, could you stop by the house and get it back to the owner?"

Casey grumbled. "Is that why I had to come in?"

Collins narrowed his gaze. "Don't be a growly pain in the ass. I even gave you coffee. I know it's inconvenient, but it's something we can do to help people. Remember? That's part of our job. We're supposed to be a team." He leaned forward and lowered his voice. "You're a good trooper, and you take the job as seriously as a heart attack, but your people skills suck. None of the others want to work with you because every fucking thing is a competition. Well, knock it off. This isn't some sort of contest to see who can have the quietest patrol district. I will tell you, you could be up for an award: asshole of the year. Whatever stick got lodged up your backside, you need to get rid of it."

"I do my job, and I do it well." Casey knew that. He took pride in doing the best damned job he could. He lived for the job. Hell, it was almost all he had.

"Yeah, you're so good that other troopers stay away. Just take the arrogance down a notch and work on getting along with your fellow troopers, because I sure as hell don't want to be writing you up for this." His gaze was rock-hard, and Casey swallowed. "You've been up for promotion, but it isn't going to happen until you are able to work with others. It's that simple." His expression softened a little. "I know you want this, and you're a good trooper, but dammit, if others won't work with you, how can you lead them?" The sergeant straightened up. "Go on and get back out there."

Casey took the coffee and left the office. He went back toward his car, making an effort to say good morning to others as he passed.

"What's with the purse? Trying out a new look?" Wyatt Nelson asked.

Casey's first instinct was to snark at him, but he swallowed it. "Just some lost property to return."

Wyatt paused in his steps. "Of course. That most definitely isn't your color, and it doesn't go with your shoes at all." He smiled and rolled his eyes. "Come on, Casey. I was only kidding. What's gotten under your skin?"

"It's nothing," Casey said gently. "Just more work than I have hours. You know how it is." Their districts were next to each other and sometimes overlapped.

"Yeah, I do. If you need backup, let me know."

"I can…." He stopped himself. His first instinct was to say he could handle things in his district just fine, as though Wyatt had been taking a dig at him. But Wyatt's open expression gave him pause. "Thanks. I appreciate the offer. You do the same." He lifted the bag in his hand. "Okay, I need to return my fashion accessory to its rightful owner." A smile crossed his lips. "I'll see you later."

Wyatt half jogged into the building, and Casey got into his patrol car. He had another break-in to investigate and the purse to return, and that was before any more reports came in—and given the way things had been going lately, more reports were inevitable. He just wished he could get a handle on these break-ins. Casey knew they were related, but there was very little to go on.

HIS FIRST stop was another robbery investigation. The story was much the same. The usual types of items had been stolen. So far he had nine incidents in the past four weeks. Casey took down the details and made notes of the similarities to the others, then left behind yet another shaken and frightened homeowner who wanted answers like Casey did.

Back in his patrol car, he took a few minutes to review his notes before heading to the address on the identification in the purse. Ten minutes later, he pulled onto the gravel two-track that led up to the house. He slowly got out of the car, taking in his surroundings. There were no cars and no human sounds. Casey wasn't sure if anyone was home until the curtains on the nearest window moved to the side and then slid back into place.

His boots crunched on the gravel, and birds sang in the nearby trees while cicadas hummed their mating song. He went up to the front door and knocked firmly, carrying the purse under his arm.

When he didn't get an answer, he knocked again, knowing people were inside. Soft footsteps behind the door told him someone was indeed home, and he was about to knock a third time when he heard locks disengaging and then the door cracked open a couple of inches.

A kid peered through the crack.

"Is your mother home?" Casey asked. He didn't get an answer. "I'm with the police, and I have her purse. Can you get her, please?" He noticed the chain was still on the door. It closed, and then after some fumbling and clinking, the door opened again.

"Mommy isn't home," a little boy about ten years old said.

"Is your dad here?" When the boy shrugged, he became concerned. "Who's home with you?"

"Mama will be back," the boy said, his voice high and pitched with fear and worry.

"It's okay. I have her purse. Is it okay if I bring it inside? I'm a policeman." He knelt down. "You know that the police are here to help you, right?" He had taught Stranger Danger classes and knew he needed to be careful. He didn't want to scare the kid, but he wondered what was really going on. While he waited, one more little face peered out from behind the boy, a small girl Casey guessed might be five or six, holding a stuffed rabbit.

"Mama says not to talk to strangers, and I'm not supposed to let anyone in the house." The young boy was scared, that was obvious, but there was something more to it.

"Let me bring in your mama's purse. I'm not going to hurt you." God, he hoped he sounded as kind and gentle as he was trying to. "Are you two home alone?"

The boy shook his head. "Beau is here too," the boy said.

Casey breathed a little easier. "How old is he?" He hoped that was the babysitter.

"Four," the boy answered.

It dawned on Casey that there were three young kids without an adult. "How long has your mommy been gone?"

The little girl began to cry. "I want Mommy," she whimpered, and the boy lowered his head.

Casey didn't make any move to go inside. "When did you see your mama last?" The boy shrugged. "Was it today?" Casey half whispered in an effort to be gentle. The boy shook his head. "Yesterday?" Another head shake. "It's okay. I'm going to help you, I promise."

Fuck, he had seen a hell of a lot of shit that people did to one another. A killing that gave him nightmares for weeks, men hitting their wives and girlfriends. Those calls got to him every time. He'd seen the worst kind of hurt, but these three kids—and he hoped there weren't more—touched his heart. After six years on the job, Casey had come to wonder if that was even possible any longer. It was easier to wall it off than to let it get battered day in and day out.

"What's your name?" Casey asked, deciding to take things really slow. "I'm Trooper Casey."

"Phillip," the boy answered softly.

Casey leaned a little closer. "And what's your name?" he asked the little girl.

"That's Jolie," Phillip answered as Jolie slunk behind him.

He wasn't going to push inside. "Have you had enough to eat?"

"I'm hungry," Jolie whispered and started crying again.

"It's okay. Do you want my help to get something to eat?" Casey asked. He held out his hand. Phillip stared at it and then took it.

Relief washed over Casey as he slowly got up and followed Phillip into the house. It was pretty clean. The house seemed to have been vacuumed and dusted recently. He did a quick sweep of the house, including checking the upstairs, before returning.

"What have you been eating?" Casey went through the living and dining areas to the kitchen. A pile of dishes—mostly plates and cups—sat in the sink.

"Peanut butter and jelly," Jolie answered as Casey opened the refrigerator. It held very little. Some condiments, a nearly empty jar of jam, a quarter of a jar of peanut butter, some pickles, and a mostly empty jug of milk. The cupboards didn't have much more, with a few boxes of macaroni and cheese and some spices. He didn't see any bread or even crackers. God, these kids were down to the very end of their food.

"Where's Beau?" Casey asked Phillip.

"Hiding," Phillip answered.

"Why don't you both go find him, and I'll make you some macaroni and cheese. Okay?" There were so many things running through his head, but he didn't want to panic the kids. They were already under enough stress. Once they hurried away, he called in and requested Wyatt's backup, got some water on the stove to get the kids fed, and then made a call to Child Services.

The kids returned with their brother in tow. Little Beau was adorable, with a head of unruly brown hair, huge brown eyes, and his thumb stuck firmly in his mouth. "Are you Beau?" Casey asked gently, and Beau nodded, leaving his thumb firmly in place. "Do you like macaroni and cheese?" He nodded again, holding Phillip's hand. "Good. Jolie said she was hungry, so I wanted to make you something to eat."

"No peanut butter?" Jolie asked, and when Casey shook his head, she grinned. "Good."

Once he got the boxed mac and cheese finished, Phillip got out what seemed to be the last of the clean dishes in the cupboard and the last clean silverware in the drawer. Once again Casey wondered how long these poor children had been in the house alone. After he got the food dished up and Phillip divided the last of the milk between them, Casey stepped out of the room to call the sergeant.

"What's going on?" the sergeant asked.

"That purse you gave me to return has opened a whole kettle of fish. I got here, and the lady it belongs to is nowhere to be found. Her three children are at the house alone, probably have been for days." He felt sick at the thought. What kind of parent did this sort of thing? "I needed you to know that this is going to take a while. I don't think they've eaten much, so I made them something to eat. Wyatt is going to be over soon, and I called Child Services."

"Good. Keep the kids calm, and find out what you can from them. Maybe we can find a relative in the area who will take them. Call in names, and I'll have people here get on it."

"Okay," Casey agreed, still a little nervous about providing unexpected child care. "All three of them are eating like they haven't had a hot meal in days."

"And idea how long they've been alone?"

"Guessing five days to a week. The poor things have eaten what they can and are nearly out of food." He spoke softly, looking out the window as Wyatt pulled up in his patrol car, followed by a dark sedan that Casey hoped was Child Services. "I'll send you any information I can get."

They ended the call, and Casey let Wyatt and Donald Ickle—the social worker from Child Services who'd driven the sedan—inside. Then he returned to the kitchen to find Phillip and Jolie at the table, but Beau missing.

"Where is he?"

"Hiding," Jolie said. "Strange men scare him. There were people in the garage a few days ago, and it scared him really bad."

"Will you check that out?" Casey asked Wyatt, who nodded.

Casey found Beau hiding in one of the cupboards. He bent down, talking softly and holding out his hand. Once Beau took it, he lifted the little boy, hugging him, surprised when Beau put his arms around his neck and held almost tightly enough to cut off his air. "Are you still hungry?" Casey asked, rubbing his back.

"Want Mama," he cried.

"I know. I'm going to try to find her for you." What the hell else was he supposed to say? "I promise. Do you want to eat some more?"

"Sit with me," Phillip said.

Beau went to his brother and sat on his lap. Casey pushed the plate over to him and swallowed hard. Then he tilted his head toward the other room, and Donald followed him.

"What have we got here?" Donald asked with a sigh.

"Mom missing for nearly a week, I'd guess. Father not around. I made them something to eat because they looked half-starved and there was little food in the house. Ummm...." He cleared his throat.

"It's okay. If these sorts of things don't get to you, then you aren't human. And believe me, I've seen worse. At least these three are fed and relatively clean. And they seem to trust you to a degree. Introduce me as Donny and tell them that I'm going to help them find their mother too."

"I'm hoping we can locate a relative that will take them," Casey said, and Donald nodded. He returned to the kitchen and introduced Donald.

"Phillip, can you tell me your last name?" He wanted to make sure that the kids had the same surname as their mother.

"Riley," he answered.

Casey wrote it down, being thorough, and it gave him a few seconds to process his horror at these kids being left alone. "Do you have an aunt or an uncle that you see?" Casey hoped Phillip would know the most information, but he shook his head. "Is there anyone you know? A cousin? Maybe a close friend of your mom's?" The kids all looked at one another blankly. "What about your grandma and grandpa?" Another shake of the head. "Do you have any relatives close by?" He was becoming a little desperate.

"There's Uncle Bertie, but Mama says he doesn't like us. Mama had a fight with him, so we don't see him anymore."

"Mama says he's mean and doesn't care," Jolie supplied.

"Is your uncle Bertie's last name Riley too?" he asked, and Phillip shrugged. Casey wrote it down anyway and hoped for the best. He messaged the sergeant with the information, along with the kids' names and ages. Maybe there were records that would help. Anything so these kids could be properly taken care of.

"You did really good," Donald told Phillip, who finished up his food and put his dishes in the nearly overflowing sink. He then helped the littler ones before they wandered into the living room, sat on the sofa, and turned on the television.

"What the…?" Casey asked Donald.

"They're fed and calm, and that's the best thing for now. Let's hope that we can find a relative who will take them. But if not, I'll make some calls."

Casey shared the information he'd gotten from the kids with Donald, who would have his own report to write.

Wyatt came inside, his expression grim. "Someone was in the garage, and it's my guess that they took whatever had any value at all. The place was pretty well cleaned out, but I have no idea what they might have gotten without the owner to tell us. I doubt the kids would know, but there was definite evidence of a break-in."

"Any sign of who might have done it? Other than things missing."

Wyatt shook his head. "I don't know. It's like stuff isn't there any longer, but that's about all. It looked like the side door was open and they got in easily."

"But they made noise, and that scared the kids," Casey said, "who may have seen something. I'm pretty sure little Beau hid, but the others might have looked outside."

"I'll ask them," Wyatt offered, but Casey put his hand on his arm, stopping him.

"No," he said gently.

"Casey's right. It should be him," Donald said and went into the living room.

Casey paused and decided that he didn't need to ask those questions at that moment. Beau sat on Phillip's lap, the older boy's arms cradling his brother. Jolie sat next to both of them, hugging the stuffed rabbit, leaning on Phillip, all three of them comforting each other. The last thing he wanted to do was add more stress with his questions.

His phone vibrated, and he left the kids with Donald and Wyatt and took the call in the kitchen. "Hey, Sarge."

"We located a relative, the uncle. His name is Bertram Riley, and he lives on East South Street in Carlisle. I'll text you the address and phone number. I suggest contacting him. See what he's willing to do."

"I will. Thank you," Casey said and then punched in the numbers from the text. He would prefer to do this in person, but showing up at the guy's front door might be more of a shock.

"Mr. Riley?" he asked once the call was answered.

"Yes…?"

"I'm Trooper Casey Bombaro with the state police. Do you know Phillip, Beau, and Jolie?" he asked, hoping to trigger something.

"Yes. They're my sister's children. Has something happened to them? Has Jenn done something?" The second question was asked as though he expected a positive answer. Then the tone changed. "Case, what happened?"

That nickname and the voice triggered an old, strong memory. Something—some*one*—he hadn't thought about in years.

"Bertie?" he asked softly. He probably should have put the pieces together before this, but the thought had never occurred to him. Just like that, memories flooded back. The two of them in class, the way Bertie couldn't seem to take his gaze off him. The lunches they had together with their group of friends. Casey pulled his attention out of the past and put it back where it belonged. "The kids are okay," he said. "But we can't locate her, and it looks like she could have been gone for as long as a week."

A sharp gasp reached through the phone, followed by near panic. "I'll be right there."

Now it was Casey's turn to feel as though the ground had shifted under his feet as his heart beat a little faster at the knowledge that he was going to see the first guy he'd fallen in love with. Casey chided himself to get his head in the game and out of this flight of fancy. But still, he couldn't stop the jolt of excitement that lingered for longer than it should.

CHAPTER 2

ALL BERTIE could think about was those kids. He hadn't laid eyes on them in nearly three years and probably wouldn't have known them if he saw them on the street. Little Beau had still been a baby, about ready to take his first steps, when a fight with Jenn had escalated into some sort of all-out war in her mind, and that seemed to be that. She had cut him off from the kids as well as herself.

Still, he looked around the flower shop. "Millie, I need to go right away. I'll be back as soon as I can. The arrangements for today's pickup are in the cooler. Just take orders and watch the shop with Jerry." Adrenaline took over. He had to get to those kids as quickly as he could.

"How long will you be gone?"

"I'm not sure. When I get back, I'll spell you for lunch. But if I'm not back, just hang a sign. Okay?" He was already halfway out the door before she agreed. He jumped into his car and took off toward Jenn's place. He drove as quickly as he dared through town and then out west into the country. Jenn always said she hated living in town, so she had found a house well away from everything. That was fine, but now it took him a while to find the place. He hadn't been there in years, but eventually he pulled into the drive next to two police cars and another vehicle. The first thing he noticed was that Jenn's car was missing.

After getting out of his car, he hurried up to the door and was met by a man in uniform. A single gaze into deep blue eyes sent a wave of recognition and buried feelings bursting to the surface. "Case, what's going on? Are the kids okay? Have you been able to find Jenn?"

"Okay, Bertie." Casey's use of his nickname was surprisingly soothing, even if his tone seemed official. "Other than unsure and scared, the kids are fine. I can go into details later, but they're okay. Jenn Riley is missing, and we don't know for exactly how long or how far she might have gotten."

"Her car is gone. If she had the same one, it was a Toyota Corolla, sort of a light green color. Always hated that thing." Case wrote it down. "What's going to happen to the kids?"

"I guess a lot of that depends on you. Child Services has been contacted and is already here. I think it's best if you talk to him. Donald will be able to help figure out the next steps." Once again, he sounded deep in police officer mode, maybe bordering on asshole. Bertie couldn't help wondering if Casey was like this all the time now.

"Can I take the kids?" Bertie asked before he could think of the repercussions. He only knew that they needed to be with family, and with their mother missing, Bertie was all they had. There was no one else. His and Jenn's parents were gone. It had been just the two of them for a number of years. "I'm all the family they have left, and I don't want them going to strangers."

"Come inside and see the kids, and then you can talk to Donald. He should be able to give you all the details you need." And just like that, Casey's eyes filled with the care and softness Bertie remembered. Up until now, they had been hard and cold, like ice. But talking about the kids, they warmed to match the sky. That was the Casey he remembered. At least that man was inside the uniform somewhere and hadn't been lost for good.

Bertie followed Casey inside and slowly approached the kids.

"Uncle Bertie?" Phillip said.

Bertie nodded, kneeling down. They had all grown since he'd seen them last, and he swallowed hard at how much of their lives he'd missed. "It's me. You remembered?" He had wondered if they would have forgotten him completely.

"Do you still have Smidgen?" Phillip asked.

Bertie grinned. "I do. He's at the store right now, and I'm sure he'll be happy to see you." Smidgen was his dog. He was almost purebred King Charles spaniel, but smaller than most. When he was a pup, Bertie had called him a little smidge of a dog, and it stuck. "You must be Jolie. You were only a few years old when I saw you last." And she looked so much like his sister at that age. "And this is Beau. I remember you as a baby." Beau immediately buried his face against Phillip.

"It's okay. That's Uncle Bertie, and he's nice."

"Mama said you were selfish and mean," Jolie said. Her eyes were exactly like her mother's.

"Do I look mean?" Bertie asked. That seemed to catch Jolie off guard. She watched him and then shook her head. "Good. Because I'm not mean or selfish. I promise." God, looking into those scared eyes made him want to cry. Where the hell was Jenn, and how could she leave them like this? Bertie wanted to think that she hadn't done it on purpose, but knowing his sister and her mental state the past few years, he wouldn't put anything past her. "Do you guys want to come to my house? You can see Smidgen, and I'll take care of you until we can find your mama."

"But what about Mama?" Jolie asked.

"It will just be until Trooper Casey can find her. Okay?" He held out his hand, and Jolie took it. "Can you go upstairs and pack something to bring with you? Bring clothes and your favorite toys."

Phillip took Beau with him, and they went upstairs. Bertie sat on the sofa, head in his hands, wondering what he was going to do.

"It will be okay," Donald said as he sat down. "The first thing you're going to need is car seats for the younger ones. I don't see any in the house, which means they were probably in her car. Phillip is big enough that he doesn't need one, but he still needs to ride in the back seat. I'll contact the office and have a colleague bring out two of them for you."

"What am I going to do with them while I'm at work?" Bertie asked.

"Let me make a few calls. I have some contacts at day care centers and will arrange temporary care for you until we know more. You wouldn't happen to know if the kids are in day care now?"

Bertie shrugged. He had no idea about the kids' lives. "Jenn cut me off years ago. She hasn't had anything to do with me."

"Do you know why?" Donald asked.

He sighed. "It's a little hard to piece together because Jenn is secretive a lot of the time. Then she lies a lot to make herself look better. But near as I can tell, she was in an accident, and that left her unconscious for a few days. Concussion. After she recovered, she was different. More suspicious and moody. I hoped it would pass, but it only got worse. I tried to convince her to get help, but she pushed me away. Then, after Beau's first birthday, I tried to get her to seek help again and she blew up at me. No one can hold a grudge like Jenn, and I haven't seen her or the kids since." He had played that over and over in his head. "All I can think of is that the concussion changed her somehow. Like those football players. But I don't know. Now she's gone and those kids need someone."

"Are you willing to take them?" Donald asked. "I know it sounds harsh, but I have to ask. I don't want to assume anything."

"Of course I am. I love them." He bit his lower lip. "Jenn doesn't even know, but I went to Phillip's school programs and concerts. I always sat in the back where Jenn didn't see me, but I looked for them. So yes. These kids are my only family, and I'm not going to turn my back on them." He knew that for sure. The rest he'd figure out.

"Okay. Let me get some paperwork done so I can put the children in your custody temporarily. Then I'll arrange for the car seats and the rest."

Donald got busy, and Bertie went upstairs to find Phillip with Beau's suitcase packed and working on his. Jolie was in her room, which was reasonably clean. She had a pink Barbie suitcase on the bed and had stuffed half her animals inside, and nothing else.

"Honey, you're going to need some clothes. Why don't you take your bunny and one other animal with you, and then we can use the suitcase to pack your clothes?" He sat on the edge of the bed. "I promise we can come back for more toys if we need them and that they'll be here when we find your mama." God, he hoped to heck they figured out what had happened.

She looked on the verge of tears, and Bertie picked her up and held her as she cried for her mama. He got the idea that he was going to be doing a lot of that over the next few days. He rocked slowly from side to side. The tears dried up, and soon enough he realized he was holding a sleeping little girl.

"Is everything okay?" Casey asked in a whisper from the doorway. "I need to get going, but you're in good hands with Donald. He's the best at what he does, and if it's okay, I'd like to stop by to ask the kids a few questions. Maybe I can do that tomorrow. The garage was broken into, and I know it scared Beau. Maybe the kids saw something."

Bertie nodded. "Of course. I work in the shop until five tomorrow, and I hope Donald can help with some sort of day care. As it is, I'll have to take the kids in with me for the rest of the day." That wasn't ideal, but he didn't have a choice. There was so much work to do, and a lot of it had been contracted from him especially. The store was very lucrative because Bertie commanded a great deal for his original one-of-a-kind designs.

Casey stepped forward and handed him a card. "I put my cell on the back. Maybe you can give me a call if you need anything—a beer, pizza, maybe a chance to catch up if you want." There was that damned smile that always made Bertie willing to follow Casey anywhere, including off a cliff if he asked. Something about this man got under his skin like no one else ever could.

"I think I'm going to need all the help I can get. And sure, stop over tomorrow to talk to the kids. That would be great, and it would give me a chance to settle them down a little and let them have some quiet time where everything isn't all mixed up." Though maybe that would be a much longer time off, but still.

"Okay. I'll see you tomorrow."

Casey left, and Bertie heard the front door of the house open and close with a soft thunk. He gently laid Jolie on the bed and did his best to pack for her. When Phillip peered in, Bertie checked with him about what he'd packed, and Phillip added a few items.

"These are her favorite shoes and her favorite shirt," he said, adding pink slippers to the suitcase along with a unicorn T-shirt.

"Would you take that downstairs for me? Once Donald returns, we'll head out. I thought we could stop at Target for coloring books, crayons, markers, and things like that. I have to work the rest of the day, but I thought you could all color and stuff in the office." It was the best he could do on short notice. "If you'd rather do something else, that's cool." Bertie had no idea what ten-year-olds did nowadays.

"Can I bring my iPad to play a game?" Phillip asked.

"Of course, and remember the charger," he said. Look at him sounding parental all of a sudden. "Once Donald comes back, we'll get ready to go."

BERTIE STOPPED at Target and held hands with Beau and Jolie as they walked through the store. Phillip pushed the cart loaded with crayons, coloring and puzzle books, plenty of snacks, and things that the kids said they liked. Bertie picked up a few games and some LEGO for all of them to use; then he drove to the shop.

"Why are we going here?" Jolie asked.

"This is where I work, and you can all sit at a table in my office and color. Phillip will be with you, and I'll be out front." He knew it wasn't ideal, but he had no other choice. There were things he had to get done. He got the kids out of the car, grabbed the bags of goodies from Target, and took the kids inside.

"Thank goodness," Millie said. "I put the orders on your work table. I'll be back in half an hour." She grabbed her purse and rushed out the door. Fortunately, Alice was the shop assistant that afternoon, and nothing fazed her.

"Who are these darlings?" she asked with a huge smile. Alice was a dear and the most grandmotherly person Bertie had ever known.

"Phillip, Jolie, and Beau. Guys, this is Alice. Let me get you all settled in the back, and then I'll be right out here. Okay?"

"Of course," Alice said as cheerfully as ever, which the kids instantly responded to. Alice already had Jolie's hand, and Phillip easily went along with her. The only one not sure was Beau, who held Bertie's hand in his version of a death grip.

"It's okay. I'll be right out here, and I'll come in whenever I can to make sure you're okay. Will you promise to be good? You can color pictures for me. Okay?" He lifted him and got them all set up at a table in the corner of the office with what he swore was enough stuff to draw and color to satisfy two kindergarten classes for a year.

Phillip played on the iPad while the others sat and colored. Bertie returned to his work table behind the front counter and repositioned it slightly so he could see in to where the kids were. Then he got to work.

He had been called an artist with flowers, using them to paint a picture, convey an emotion, make the viewer feel something. His work wasn't about making wedding bouquets or funeral arrangements, though he had done both and still did. But when he worked, it was to convey the joy or the solemnity of the occasion. Bertie's arrangements had stood pride of place in the state capitol, at gubernatorial inaugurations. He had even had arrangements presented at national museums. And that was what he put into every piece he did.

The first thing Bertie did was consult his designs, and then he got down to work. He could almost see the arrangement in his mind even before he began. Like always, he tended to sink into his head as he worked. He got the flowers exactly where he wanted them, reflexing some of the petals to make them seem larger. This piece had a very modern shape and aesthetic, with hard lines rather than curves, in deep colors, with some accents in black, some the color of stainless steel. It was a study in contradictions—soft flowers, yet the arrangement itself was hard.

In a way, it reminded him of Casey. Not in the look, of course, but how it made him feel. And Casey got his heart racing, even as his mind screamed not to jump in—that things weren't the way they had been years ago. In college, they had been carefree kids, just starting out. Learning their way, feeling the path forward.

The overall effect was striking, and once he was done with the flowers, he added the tag, completed the ticket, and then placed the arrangement in the cooler. Stepping back, he took a final look at his creation as it reflected his inner turmoil back at him.

"How can you do that?" Millie asked when she returned from lunch, interrupting his momentary musing. "You take some of the ugliest flowers and make them into something so beautiful." Millie was very much a traditionalist, but she was a fan of his work, even when it wasn't her style. To Bertie, that was a sign that he had done his job well.

"The customer gave me basic parameters, and I went from there," he answered, not wanting to talk about what had *really* brought the muse forward. The hot-and-cold-running Casey he'd seen made him wonder what had happened to the smiley, happy man he'd known, and it flashed caution in front of his eyes. Bertie had seen his sister's moods rise and fall in seconds, and he was still living the aftermath of that roller coaster.

When he poked his head into the office, Jolie got up from the table and hurried over.

"What's wrong?" he asked.

"I gotta go," she stage-whispered.

"Do you want Millie to take you?" Bertie asked.

She shook her head and took his hand. So for the first time in his life, Bertie took a little girl to the bathroom. He suspected that he was going to be doing a lot of firsts over the next few days, and he was going to need to be sure he was up for it.

BERTIE MANAGED to keep his head above water for the rest of the day, with his work and the kids. Thankfully, Millie helped keep an eye on them. But by the time he was ready to go, they were restless and filled with energy. So he stopped at McDonald's for food and took them to LeTort Park, where they ate, and then the kids could run around the play structure while he sat outside at a picnic table in the shade.

"Bertie?"

He looked away from the kids as Casey strode across the grass.

"What are you doing here?" Casey took off his intimidation sunglasses, and the words sounded less like an interrogation.

"The kids needed a chance to run off energy, and I needed a few minutes outside to try to think. What brings you here?"

"I live over there at the other end of the trail into the park. I walk here a lot of evenings." He sat down on the bench across from him. "How are the kids doing?"

"Right now they're fine. But I suspect that the questions and worries will have built up enough that some kind of meltdown is imminent. Donald found me a day care for the kids. Jenn, it seems, gets disability, and that is what they have been living on. It isn't a huge amount, but she's been staying home with them." All of this was just more change heaped onto frightened children.

"I'm glad we were able to find you," Casey said.

"Me too." He turned back to where the kids were playing, wanting to look somewhere other than Casey's eyes, because dammit, it would be so easy to get drawn into them. There were questions he wanted to ask, but Bertie wasn't sure he had the right to ask them, so the silence between them drew on. He wasn't sure what to say.

"Did you stay in school?" Casey finally asked.

"Yes. I studied art and design and became a florist. I manage Wilmont's Abundance over on York Road. I also work as the chief designer for them. How about you?" Casey had sort of disappeared after one semester, and Bertie never knew what happened.

"Things didn't work out too well in school for me. What little money I had ran out, so I joined the Navy. Mom and Dad were proud and all, but I hated it. Found out that I don't like ships. They're way too confining, and the entire time I was on one, all I wanted to do was get the hell off. But there was no place to go. So once my tour was over, I didn't re-up and decided to give school another try. I went to the academy and did really well. I love working for the state police. I don't have to sit in an office, and my days are always different."

"I remember that about you." Casey always seemed to have so much energy that he could barely sit still in class. "Honestly, I would have thought that the Navy would have been a good fit. You had so much enthusiasm and energy back then."

"It probably would have if I hadn't spent my quiet hours wondering what the hell I'd do if the ship sank. I was fine when I was busy, but it was something I had to force myself not to do or I'd go crazy. A friend asked me to go on a cruise a few years ago, but there was no way in hell I could even think about it. I never want to set foot on a ship again." And there was that wicked smile and brightness in Casey's eyes. "It wasn't really that bad, I guess. The food was decent, and I was busy a lot of the time. I don't think it was the best fit for me, but I had no idea I'd feel that way. How about you? Do you love what you do?"

"Without a doubt. I work with flowers all day, and at the house I have amazing gardens and a ton of flowers blooming all the time. I grow some of my own vegetables." He turned as Jolie hurried out of the play area. She raced over, and Bertie hugged her when she got close.

"I got sand in my eye," she whimpered.

"Okay. Can I look?" Bertie asked. She turned her face upward, keeping her eye closed. "Blink a few times for me." She did. "Does it feel better?" She blinked again and nodded, a tear running down her cheek. "You're such a big girl, and you did really good. I think the sand is gone now." He kissed the top of her head.

"Can I go play again?"

"Sure, honey. Tell the others that we have to leave in about ten minutes," Bertie told her, and she ran back at full speed, all the energy in the world.

"Do you have any idea where their mother might have gone?" Casey asked.

"I wish I had a clue. Her car is missing." He paused. "Look, Jenn had her issues, I know that. But I don't think she would have willingly left the kids and just run away or something. She didn't make the best decisions in her life. Hell, she could compound dumb on top of stupid so damned fast, but she loved those kids with everything she had, and my heart is telling me she didn't just walk away from them."

"We have to look at all possibilities. We have a bulletin out statewide for her car. We figure that will be the easiest way for us to find her, but if she left the state, then we aren't going to have an easy way to find her unless we get federal help. I'm hoping it doesn't come to that. We have checked hospitals for someone under her name or a Jane Doe that meets her description, but so far we have nothing."

Bertie sighed. "That's a relief. At least she isn't hurt." Though the thought occurred to him that something worse could have happened to her and he would have no way of knowing. "But...."

"Don't jump to any conclusions. I know it's hard, but there are a lot of possibilities, and we have to run each of them down," Casey told him. "Is there anyplace she might run to if she needed a break? Or somewhere she'd go if she were in trouble? Maybe somewhere nearby that she used to visit as a kid?" Casey asked. "Anywhere that was special."

Bertie tried to think. "Nowhere she'd go without the kids." He kept coming back to the fact that she had left the kids behind. That was something that kept bothering him. Jenn wasn't the greatest mother in the world. She had a tendency to be selfish at times, and since her injury, that tendency had become more pronounced. But he still didn't see her taking off, leaving them alone at home.

Phillip came out with the other two. Jolie hurried over, climbed onto the bench, and drank the last of her soda. Beau climbed into Bertie's lap, and he held the cup for him so he could get a drink.

"Are you ready to go?" Bertie asked.

"Did you find Mommy yet?" Jolie asked Casey.

"Not yet. But I will do my best. I promise." He turned to Phillip. "When your mom left, did she say where she was going?"

Phillip thought a minute. "To the store."

"Do you know which one?" Casey asked. Phillip shook his head. "It's okay. I was hoping you might have remembered."

"To get food, I guess," he answered. "Maybe cigarettes. She was out and not very happy." Phillip finished his soda.

"Let's go to my house so you can all get settled for the night. Okay?" God, Bertie was so worked up. He wasn't sure how he was going to sleep all the kids, but they'd figure it out one way or another. His house wasn't all that big.

"Come on, let's go get into the car," Phillip said and took the others off toward where Bertie had parked.

"That kid is ten going on thirty," Casey commented. "Believe it or not, he gave us a few avenues to use to try to track her down. I'll see you tomorrow, and I'll call if we find out anything at all. I promise."

THE KIDS were just as wound up when he got them home. Beau ran around the living room, and Jolie danced, her shoes tapping on Bertie's hardwood floors, while Smidgen raced and wagged his tail right along with their playing. "All right, you two, let's get you upstairs and into your pajamas," Bertie said.

The house had three bedrooms, and he used one as a work and craft room. Still, that room had a pull-out sofa, and he figured Phillip could stay in there. The other two could share the bed in the guest room. At least he hoped that would work. After getting some things moved around in his craft room, he found Jolie and Beau using the guest-room bed as a trampoline. He caught Beau and whisked him down onto the floor.

"Let's get our jammies on. Jolie, do you need help?"

"I can do it." She climbed down, opened her suitcase, and dumped everything out onto the floor. She picked up her nightgown and ran to the bathroom, then closed the door. At least Beau was neater, and Bertie helped him get his pajamas on before picking up Jolie's clothes and setting her suitcase aside. Then he closed the curtains to darken the room, and Beau climbed into bed after brushing his teeth and using the bathroom. Once Jolie joined them, Bertie got her settled as well. Beau hugged a stuffed dinosaur and Jolie her rabbit. Fortunately, they were tired, and after Bertie told them a story, they went right to sleep. The poor darlings seemed worn out. Smidgen jumped up at the foot of the bed and lay down facing them as though he intended to watch and make sure they were okay. He was a good dog and really seemed to love the kids, which was a relief.

Bertie was nearly as tired as they were. He went downstairs to where Phillip sat on the sofa with his iPad. "I need to get your bed made up," Bertie said before sitting in a chair with a sigh.

"Is Mom going to come back?" Phillip asked.

He thought for a second and was ready to give him a standard answer, but the look in Phillip's eyes stopped the words. This kid needed to know the truth. "I have no idea. I know they're going to try to find her. I wish I had some idea where she is, but I don't. They have as much information as we can give them, and finding people is part of what the police do." He stood back up, because if he didn't do what he needed to, he was going to fall to sleep right where he was. Leaving Phillip on the sofa, Bertie made himself a cup of tea and took it with him upstairs, where he made up the bed for Phillip and checked on the sleeping little angels.

"They're out," he told Phillip when he got back downstairs and finally relaxed a little in his chair. Bertie wasn't sure if he was cut out for this, but he was damned well going to try. His phone dinged with a message from Donald, giving him the address of a day care a few blocks away. He thanked him and was about to put his phone down when a message came through from Casey.

Everything okay?

Bertie smiled. *The two youngest are in bed, and I'm exhausted. But things are okay. Any luck finding Jenn?* he responded.

We're running down some leads. How's Phillip? Is he doing okay? How are you with all this?

Bertie smiled to himself. *I think we're all holding it together for now, and that's all we can ask for. Phillip is quiet right now, but I expect more questions and a lot of hurt to build pretty soon.* He sent the message. *I know we'll be okay one way or another.* There was little he could do other than care for the kids and hope Jenn was located soon. *We'll see you tomorrow.* He set his phone aside and thought about turning on the television.

"Why don't you go on up to bed?" Bertie said to Phillip, and Phillip set his iPad aside to charge and headed for the stairs. Bertie was about to close his eyes when Phillip returned, leaning over the chair. He hugged Bertie tightly and then went upstairs to bed.

Bertie tried not to think about the sudden changes in his life. The kids, Casey, Jenn being missing. All of it seemed to pile on all at once, and there was little he could do about any of it. Having the kids back in his life was a good thing, and he was grateful for that. But Jenn's disappearance nearly a week ago… God. The thought of those little ones being alone chilled him to the bone. She was missing, and his niece and nephews were in his house and back in his life… for the time being. Yet the strangest thing was Casey's reappearance in his life, and he didn't know what to make of that. He sighed and got up, locked the doors, and turned out the lights. He might as well go to bed himself. He was going to need to get the kids dressed and to the day care in the morning before he went off to work.

Phillip seemed too old for something like that, but on such short notice, Bertie had very little alternative. Maybe he could see if there were programs at the Y or something that Phillip could attend to be with kids his own age. Bertie sent a message to Donald to get his thoughts and then cleaned up before climbing into bed in a T-shirt and boxers in case the kids got up in the middle of the night.

Not that he expected to get a lot of sleep. Just knowing the kids were in the house kept him awake until well after midnight. Finally he dropped off with the hope that he'd have enough energy to get through the following day.

CHAPTER 3

CASEY PULLED up in front of Bertie's house. Though the man he knew had definitely changed, and regardless of the fascination that meeting Bertie again had rekindled, now was not the most advantageous time to explore the feelings that seeing him raised.

He had always thought of Bertie as the one who got away. Or more accurately, the baby he had thrown out with the proverbial bathwater. His friendship with Bertie had been one of the casualties of his decision to leave school and join the Navy. In hindsight, it had been a rushed decision made because he needed to get away from his rigid parents, who saw only what they wanted. First they had pushed him to go to school, and then they had pressed for him to study what they wanted. Not that it mattered in the end. College hadn't been right for him, at least not at that point in his life. But by choosing to join the military, he had gotten away from his folks and expectations he hadn't wanted, only to leave behind the one friend who meant something to him… and all for something that hadn't fit in the first place.

"Hi, Jolie," he said as she opened the door with Bertie right behind her.

"Did you find Mommy yet?" she asked, her eyes huge and bright, so much hope in her voice.

"Not yet. But I have a bunch of people helping me," he answered, wishing he had better news. "Do you like it here with Uncle Bertie?" He thought he might try changing the subject.

Jolie nodded. "Want Mommy, though," she said, hugging her rabbit. Bertie picked her up and did his best to soothe her as he unlocked the screen door so Casey could come inside.

The house smelled amazing, and Casey inhaled deeply. "What are you making?" he asked Beau as he ran in from the kitchen, where Casey could see Phillip watching what was on the stove.

"Sketti," Beau said happily. Bertie took his hand and led them back into the kitchen and got the kids settled at a table covered with coloring books and crayons. Beau settled easily, but Jolie still fussed until Bertie set her down and got her started on another picture. He looked haggard and tired.

"I need to get them fed, and then we can sit down and go over what you need to," Bertie said as he got out bowls and things for the kids. Apparently Beau didn't want sauce, and Jolie only a little, while Phillip made up his own. Bertie sat with them while they ate.

Casey pulled out a chair. "I was hoping that maybe you could help me." He spoke gently. "You guys were so brave and a big help. You said that you heard someone in the garage."

Phillip nodded. "Yes. There were men in there, and it scared Beau really bad. He hid under the bed, and Jolie sat with me until they left." He stopped eating.

"You all did great. Really, I promise. Something like that would be scary for me."

"Me too," Bertie said.

"But you're huge," Jolie told him. "You can't be scared."

"Everyone gets scared, even me. What's important is that you protect the people who need it, the way Phillip did for you and Beau." He wanted them to be as comfortable as possible. "Did you see the men in the garage?" It hadn't escaped him that Phillip had used the plural.

Phillip lowered his gaze to the table.

"None of you are going to be in trouble. I promise," Bertie said, so gently. Damn, that tone clicked up Casey's memory. "What you're doing is helping Casey and the police."

"I seed them," Jolie said. "Phillip said to hide in the bathroom, but I sneaked out and looked." She seemed pale, and Bertie lifted her onto his lap.

"It's okay. Just tell Casey what you saw." He hugged her, and Jolie pressed her face to Bertie's shoulder.

"Can you tell me how many men there were?" Casey asked, and Jolie held up two fingers. "That's so good. You're a brave girl." Bertie stroked her hair.

"Did you see anything else?" Bertie asked. "What did the men look like?" She shrugged and held Bertie tighter. It wasn't like he was going to get a detailed description from her. "Were they wearing jeans?" he asked, and she shook her head. "Pants?"

"They had leather on," Phillip said. "Like for riding motorcycles." He was still looking down at the table. "I looked when I got Jolie to come back with me. Their clothes were dark, and they had chains on them too."

Now they were getting somewhere. "Did you see their faces? What color hair?" he asked, but Phillip shrugged. "Were they wearing boots?" Once again Phillip shrugged, and Jolie continued holding on to Bertie for dear life.

"Did they come in a car?"

"A truck," Jolie said. "It was red with stripes and a big thing on the front. It was scary." She buried her face once more, and Casey wondered if he could narrow down what the design had been, but it seemed Phillip hadn't seen it, and Jolie wasn't able to provide anything more. Still, it was more than he had before.

"You did great. Both of you," Casey said with a huge smile. "Really good."

"Me too?" Beau asked, and Casey ruffled his hair.

"You were all amazing." He pulled out his pad and made notes on what the kids had told him about the vehicle's description, and that the men wore leathers, which indicated the possibility of motorcycles part of the time. Clearly they had dressed that way so they wouldn't be seen.

"Why don't you finish your dinner, and then you can watch cartoons," Bertie said.

Jolie returned to her seat and ate some more of her dinner. Phillip seemed reticent, watching both Casey and Bertie for some sort of sign.

"You were all so awesome." Bertie went around and hugged each of the kids, making sure they all knew he was talking to them.

"Do you think the bad men scared Mommy away?" Jolie asked.

"Oh, honey," Bertie said. "I think that the two things are separate, but Casey isn't going to stop looking for your mom. I promise you that."

Casey nodded. He had no reason to believe that the robbery had anything to do with Jenn's disappearance. If anything, it was tied to the series of robberies in that area of the county. Heck, he *hoped* they were related because he had finally gotten some information on the robbers and they hadn't found much about Jenn. Only time and investigation would tell.

"I should probably leave you and the kids alone," Casey said as Bertie made up a plate and set it in front of him.

"Eat," Bertie told him. "Your stomach has been rumbling for the last ten minutes."

Casey knew better than to argue with Bertie and pulled a chair up to the table. Bertie got him a glass of ice water, and he tucked into the pasta.

"Did you make the sauce?" Casey asked as intense flavor burst on his tongue. There was no way this came from a jar—it had too much flavor and zest for that.

"Of course I did. My grandma taught me how to make her sauce before she died. She didn't even tell Mama, but she showed me. When I make it, I put enough in the freezer that I can thaw it out whenever I need a quick meal." He ate his own dinner, and Casey could almost believe that they were a family sitting down to eat. Only, of course, they weren't. It was a weird sensation that Casey didn't understand the root of. Honestly, he had never given any thought to having a family. He knew he was too grouchy a lot of the time to actually find someone who would care for him. No one could get past his prickly exterior. And the question of having kids was certainly not something he'd given any thought to.

"It's really good," Casey said as he continued eating. It had been a hellaciously long day, and the food and company were nice. Casey lowered his gaze when someone patted his leg. Casey lifted Beau onto his lap and finished eating as he held the youngster.

"It looks like you made a friend already," Bertie said with a smile.

Jolie was still wary, and Casey figured it might take him finding her mommy for her to come around. Still, this was nice. "Can I color?" Jolie asked, and Bertie set her down. She hurried off, and soon enough Beau followed his sister. Only Casey and Bertie remained at the table once Phillip headed off to use his iPad.

"Is there any news at all?" Bertie asked now that the kids were out of immediate earshot.

"I think I tracked her to a grocery store on the west side of Carlisle. She gets food assistance, and we were able to trace a transaction to that store. So we know she was there a week ago, but there hasn't been anything since, and we haven't found her car, which concerns me, because that means she could have left the state. I have the entire department on the lookout statewide, and I figured we'd locate it pretty quickly if the car were out and about." Casey was afraid she might have left the state or ended up in a remote ravine. Or worse, took off north, which meant driving over one of the mountain ranges and going off the mountain. The overgrowth was thick in many places, so the car would disappear. There was also the possibility that something nefarious had happened to her.

"What concerns me is Jenn's mental state. I haven't asked the kids because I don't want them to think that I don't like their mother, but what if she was off her meds or trying to self-medicate? Since the accident, her state of mind could be extreme, and I know she was on meds, but I don't know what they were or if she was taking them."

"We found some medications in the bathroom, but the prescription dates seemed old." Maybe she had gone off them. "But that doesn't change any of the possible outcomes. Does she have any friends?"

Bertie shrugged. "I have no idea. You could try her neighbors. But after three years, I don't know who might still be in her life. Jenn tended to make friends easily, and then they tended to disappear after a while. I suspect because she would get anxious and really selfish, and folks don't stick around for a lot of that kind of behavior." He sighed, frustration rolling off him. "I don't know what to do. This is how it always was. Mom and Dad favored Jenn. She was the younger sister, so I was supposed to stick up for her, and she got away with nearly everything. She'd make a mess, and Mom and Dad would try to clean it up. Now she's made another mess, and I feel like I have to have the answers. But I don't know where to look or how to begin to fix this one." Bertie's face grew red.

"Breathe," Casey said gently. "Just take a deep breath and then another. Relax. You can't have all the answers, and your job for now is to take care of these kids. It's mine to try to find her. What I think I need to do is go back to the house and see if I can find a date book or something with her contacts in it."

"What about her phone?" Bertie asked. "Did you have any luck with it?"

"No. I haven't been able to locate it. I've contacted the local carriers. She has Verizon, and they say the phone isn't attached to the network," Casey explained. "Maybe we'll get lucky and find something else in the house."

"Do whatever you need to," Bertie told him. "I'm probably going to need to take the kids over to get a few more things."

"Do you want to meet me there? Maybe between us we can find something." Casey wasn't sure what he might be looking for. A date book was the obvious thing, but Bertie had known her better, and Phillip might be able to tell if something was missing. He really was beginning to get frustrated. People rarely disappeared so completely and with so little trace. Usually they left a trail, even if it was inadvertent, but Jenn seemed to have disappeared, almost in a puff of smoke.

"We can do that after work tomorrow." Bertie seemed wound as tight as a drum. Not that Casey could blame him. He was now caring for three kids, his sister was missing, and his life had been turned upside down in a matter of a day. "I'll pick up the kids, and then we can head over."

"Maybe after we check out the house, I can return the favor and make you dinner?" Casey was a decent cook, and after Bertie fed him, it was the least he could do.

"That would be nice." Bertie yawned just as Beau yelled from his place in front of the coffee table, yanking something away from Jolie, who began to cry and raced over to Bertie.

"What happened?" Bertie asked.

"She took my picture," Beau said indignantly, going right back to coloring.

"But I wanted to color the unicorn." She pushed out her lower lip. "Now it's ruined. He scribbled all over it like a big baby." She turned her head to Bertie's shoulder.

"You need to be nice to your brother," Bertie told her. "He's smaller than you, and did he have the book first?" God, he was so patient. Casey wondered where that came from as he spoke gently to Jolie, calming her while not giving in either. It was a pretty amazing sight. "You both need to share. Okay, Jolie?" he asked, and she nodded.

"Beau… you need to share. Can you do that?" Beau turned, looking at Bertie like he was from Mars. Then he pushed some of the coloring books to Jolie's side of the table. "That's a big boy." He set Jolie down, and she went back to the table, the fight quickly forgotten as they now sat quietly, Smidgen watching from beside the table as intently as if they were going to drop food to him at any moment.

"How do you find the energy?" Casey asked.

Bertie shrugged. "I don't know. I just have to." He smiled at the small pair and pushed the dishes away from his place, then put his head down on the table with an audible sigh. His dog came over, nails clicking on the floor, and Bertie pushed the chair back and lifted him onto his lap. He probably needed the comfort, and Smidgen loved the attention. "I didn't get to see these kids the last few years, and I'm realizing I missed quite a bit. Beau was one when I last saw him. Now he's four, and he didn't know me before yesterday."

"But he knows you now," Casey said gently, sliding his hand over Bertie's back. "And he isn't likely to forget you, no matter what happens." He made small circles, and Bertie sighed again, some of the tension easing out of him.

Casey liked being close to Bertie, and it surprised him how comfortable and at ease he felt with him. There was none of his need to keep his distance and be so damned careful around him like he felt with everyone else. Professional detachment had never been an issue because he largely felt that way about most people. But not Bertie. Casey sat quietly with him for a few minutes until Beau got up from the table and started running from room to room, yelling.

"What are you playing?" Bertie asked as Beau flew by.

"Race car," Beau answered before taking off again. Around and around he went until Phillip grabbed him.

"Dude, give it a rest," Phillip growled, and Beau began to whine and then cry. But that didn't last long, as soon enough he was up doing his race car imitation once again. The next time around, Bertie snagged him up into his arms.

"Please don't run in the house. I don't want you to fall and get hurt, okay? Do you want to watch TV before you get ready for bed?"

"Dora?" Beau asked, and Bertie carried him into the other room, found Dora on demand, and started an episode. Jolie went in as well, and Phillip announced that he was going up to his room. At least it grew quiet, and Casey cleared the table, put the dishes in the sink, and let Bertie sit for a while.

"Sometimes I wonder if I'm completely crazy, thinking I can care for these kids. I'm not a parent. I'm a gay florist who lives alone and works himself half to death most of the time." Bertie held his head in his hands. "Can I really do this?"

"Like you said, you can because you have to. These three need you," Casey said, trying to put himself in their place. If something like this had happened to him when he was a kid, he would have wanted someone like Bertie to take care of him.

"I know." He closed his eyes and sighed. "I just don't know if I can do it."

Casey leaned closer. "I know you can. You were always able to do anything you put your mind to. It was what made you a success in school and why you're so good at your job. And you'll be a good caretaker for the kids." He patted Bertie's shoulder and then pulled his hand away. He could get way too used to touching Bertie, and he didn't have the right to, no matter how much he loved the sleek hardness under his clothes or how much he wondered how his full lips might taste. Casey knew life sometimes threw curveballs, but he had been so stupid to let Bertie slip from his life all those years ago. He couldn't help wondering how different his life would be or how different he'd be if he hadn't. Not that he could do anything about that now.

"I wanna watch…," Beau cried. He hurried into the room in tears and went right up to Bertie. "Mommy…." He whimpered as Bertie took him into his arms.

"What happened?"

"Want Mommy," he said softly.

Bertie held him, rocking slowly. "I know, sweetheart, and we're trying to find her." He continued rocking until Beau quieted. "Do you want to watch more Dora?" He stood when Beau nodded, and Casey figured it was time for him to go. The television began playing the theme, and the kids were quiet. "Just one more episode and then it's time to get ready for bed." Bertie seemed relieved at the idea.

He came back in, and Casey stood to meet him. "You have enough to do, so I'll say good night, and I'll see you at the house tomorrow." He was hoping for some sort of lead on where Jenn might be. Anything would help.

"Okay." Bertie seemed tired, his eyes heavy. He saw Casey to the door, and Casey wasn't sure where the impulse come from, but he found himself leaning forward to kiss him but stopped himself. It didn't matter if he wanted to taste those lips. He needed to get himself together. "I'll see you tomorrow," Bertie said softly, closing the door behind him.

Casey went out to his car, but he stopped at the driver's door, looking back toward the small row house, smiling for a second as the lights shifted through the front window, Bertie's silhouette moving across the curtains. He got into the car and drove away, heading to his empty home.

STANDING OUT in front of Jenn's house, Casey waited as Bertie's car pulled into the drive. He stopped and helped the kids get out. Casey had already tried tracing Jenn from where the bag had been found, but no one had seen her. Beau raced across the dry yard and banged on the front door. "Mommy!" he cried. Jolie raced up behind him, both kids calling for their mother.

Bertie used a set of keys with a worn plastic tag to unlock the house, and the little kids raced inside with Phillip following behind.

"She isn't here, is she?" Phillip asked.

Bertie shook his head as they went inside, the younger kids calling out for their mom as they hurried through the house to find her. Bertie went to try to get them to settle down, and Casey found him a few minutes later in what had to be Jenn's room, each sitting on the bed on either side of Bertie, who held them both, talking softly while they cried.

"Come on," Bertie said, lifting Beau and taking Jolie's hand. "Let's go get a few more toys for each of you." He left the room, and Casey pulled on gloves and started going through the room. He wasn't sure what he expected to find. He was hoping he'd know it when he saw it.

Casey started with the dresser, looking over the papers and bottles on top. It all looked like everything had been set there because it was convenient. He sifted through them before going through the drawers, which held nothing but clothes. Under the bed he found dust, and he was about to check the closet when Phillip came in.

"Is there anything missing from in here?" Casey asked. "I'm trying to find something, anything, that might help us figure out where your mom might be." He opened the door to a jumbled mess that wasn't likely to tell him anything.

"No. Her coat is gone, but I know she took that with her," Phillip said softly. "This room looks the same."

"What about anywhere else in the house? Is there something gone or something that shouldn't be there?" Casey stepped back to survey the room for anything out of place, which was a futile gesture, given how disorganized everything was.

"I don't know," Phillip said. Casey checked her bathroom, once again looking at the prescription bottles. They were old, with pills still in them.

"Mama said she didn't need those anymore," Phillip told Casey. "She said that she was getting better and that the pills made her fuzzy." Casey put the bottle back. At least that might answer one question. Jenn was likely off her meds, which could lead to erratic behavior.

"That was a help. Thank you," Casey told Phillip as he left the room and wandered through the rest of the house. It wasn't dirty, just disorganized, almost chaotic. Still, he wandered slowly, picking up bags and looking through them before setting them down. Jenn had a ton of fabric bags of different kinds and sizes, some with various craft projects in them and others filled with papers and still more bags. A pink floral bag sat next to the arm of the sofa, near the wall. He lifted it out and found it full of notebooks, pens, and markers.

"That must be her art stuff. Jenn always loved to draw and things," Bertie said as he sat on the sofa next to Casey. Some of the notebooks were pencil drawings, others colored markers. Still more were filled with writing.

"Is that her story?" Bertie asked. "Jenn always said she was writing a book. But this is so jumbled it's unreadable." He took it, peered through some of the pages, then handed it back. "It's not a diary or anything."

"No date book?" Casey asked, and Bertie shook his head. It was an old-fashioned notion, but Casey had still been hopeful. He put everything back in the bag and set it where he'd found it.

"She's been gone almost ten days. She could be anywhere by now," Bertie said. "I know that people gone this long...." He swallowed hard. Casey knew it too.

"She was off her meds. Phillip told me she said she didn't need them anymore, and the containers upstairs are indeed months old, with pills still in them. Is it possible she could be off on some psychotic episode?" he asked, almost to himself. "Though people like that are usually found pretty easily because they don't hide their tracks." Sometimes they became paranoid—that could be what was happening here.

"There was nothing in the kitchen. I did clean out the trash because the kids had left a bit of a mess, but I didn't find anything in there either that might give us a clue." Bertie sighed. "Maybe we have to accept that either she's gone and doesn't want to be found or that something has happened to her. I still doubt she'd just leave the kids. She's many things, but Jenn loves her kids."

Casey was about to counter his argument when his phone chimed. He got up and left the room to return the call from the station. "Hey, Maria," he said once he had dispatch.

"Got a message for you from Wyatt. Seems they found Jennifer Riley's car. He sent over the report, and I'm forwarding it to you. It was found abandoned to the north of Carlisle in a wooded area. Wyatt is on the scene, and he's going to go over the vehicle now and will be in touch as soon as he's done. He said to tell you that there is no sign of the driver. She was not in or around the vehicle."

"Thanks for letting me know. Does he want me to join him?" Casey asked.

"It's not necessary. Wyatt said he has things in hand, and it's going to take you a while to get there. A tow truck has already been called, and you can take a look at the car with him tomorrow at the lot." She was as efficient as always.

"Thank you." Well, that answered one question. "Did he say how long he thought it had been there?"

"About a week or so. He said some of the damaged foliage started to turn brown, so it wasn't recent." She ended the call, and Casey put his phone back in his pocket. So Jenn had left and gone north after the store. It was possible that she had even come back by the house and just kept going, continued up the mountain, and lost control of the car. It seemed really strange to him, and Casey wondered why she would just pass by the house. He texted Wyatt to ask if there were groceries in the car and got an answer that there were.

I'll send you the images, but there was melted ice cream all over the back seat, dripped down the seat.

He made a call to Wyatt right away. "Does the ice cream look like it was melted when she went off the road, or was it frozen and then melted?"

"The car was at an angle, and it ran all down the seat. Why?" Wyatt asked.

"So it was still frozen. If it had been melted first, it would have splattered everywhere. Instead, it was in a mass and then melted down the seat. That means she went off the road not long after leaving the store." That told him part of what happened, but it didn't give any clue as to where she was now.

"I'll send you copies of everything we gather," Wyatt promised, and Casey hung up, still trying to make sense of this.

"What happened?" Bertie asked.

"They found the car, but not your sister. It was empty. She went off the road north of here." He was going to have to look at the car in the morning once it was towed and brought to the yard. "Maybe there's something inside that can tell us more." God, he hoped so. Though a number of possibilities ran through his head, he didn't share them with Bertie. Everything was too speculative. At least he had another piece of the puzzle. Jenn had left the house, stopped at the store, and then on her way back seemed to go by the house and just kept going. Why, he had no idea, and what caused her to go off the road was yet to be discovered.

Since there was no sign of her in or around the car, it was likely she had somehow walked away from the accident. That in itself was good, but where was she?

"I see," Bertie said. "What else?"

Casey didn't think the house was going to show him anything. More and more, Casey figured that something had happened after she'd left the house. He had no idea what. But she did go to the store like she told the kids. "We'll have to see." Right now there were no further answers. "Let's get the kids, and you can follow me to my place and I'll make dinner." There was nothing here that was going to tell him anything more.

Bertie nodded. "Phillip," he called up the stairs. "Come on, kids. We need to go and get some dinner." Phillip came down with Jolie in hand. "Where's Beau?"

Phillip shrugged, and Jolie shook her head. "Maybe he's hiding," she offered.

Bertie went upstairs and began looking through each room, and Casey joined him.

"Beau?" he asked softly in each room, listening carefully. When Bertie stuck his head in Jenn's room, soft sniffles reached Casey's ears. Bertie peered around the furniture and then bent down, looking under the bed. Beau was pressed up against the wall, lying flat on his belly. "Come on out," he said gently.

"I can't find Mama," he said, still crying. Casey wanted to wrap the little boy in comfort and try to explain that they were doing everything they could to find her. Bertie extended his hand under the bed and held still.

"I'm here for you," Bertie said and waited. Finally, he gently tugged Beau out from under the bed and sat on the edge and held him. Beau turned to Bertie, burying his face in his neck, crying his little eyes out. All Bertie kept saying over and over was that it was going to be okay and that he loved him, rocking softly until Beau's tears died away. "Are you hungry?" Bertie asked, and Beau nodded.

"Then how about we go to Mr. Casey's? He said he was going to make us dinner, and then we can get ice cream. Okay?"

"Chocolate?" Beau asked. Casey smiled and nodded. He loved that little boy already.

"Any flavor you want," Bertie said and got up, carrying Beau downstairs. Casey followed him down, and they bundled the kids into Bertie's car. Once Bertie locked up the house, Casey got in his cruiser and led the way home.

"Wow," Bertie said once he had parked in front of the row home just off the center of Carlisle. Casey had painted it up nicely, with navy blue shutters against the red brick. "I love the flower boxes."

Casey grinned. "I did them myself. They don't get sunlight because it's north-facing, so I use impatiens and ferns in them. The ones on the second-floor windows get some sun, but I use the same flowers and water them from the windows upstairs." Casey unlocked the door and ushered them inside.

"Guys, you need to behave. Okay?" Bertie said as soon as they stepped inside.

"The furniture is leather and really durable. They aren't going to hurt anything." Once he'd locked the door, Casey set his keys in the bowl on the side table. "Now what do you want for dinner? I have chicken nuggets, mac and cheese, and hot dogs."

"Nuggets, please," Phillip said. Jolie couldn't seem to decide, and Beau wanted a hot dog.

"Then I can make nuggets and hot dogs. Okay?" He went through to the kitchen and got started, putting the chicken into the air fryer. Casey made a quick fruit salad with berries he'd found at the market.

"Oh my God," Bertie said, and Casey smiled. "Did you build the glass room?"

"No. The house had the conservatory on the back. It's quite old, and I love it. I bought the house because of it, and that way I can raise my orchids." He was really proud of his babies.

"These are gorgeous," Bertie said, standing in front of the glass room, staring at the wrought iron benches with glass tops that went around the three sides of the space and then the glass shelves higher up. All were filled with pots holding orchids, nearly every color of the rainbow. "You never told me you were into flowers." He gasped again. "Did you do the backyard?"

"Yes. It was just grass when I moved in. I did the patio and hardscaping first before adding the plantings. It's mostly shade, so I designed all the plants around leaf color, size, and shape." He was pretty proud of it. "We can eat out there if you want," Casey offered. The kids seemed excited.

"Now, you have to be careful when you're out there, because you don't want to hurt Anthony and Cleopatra. They're the box turtles that live in the yard." Casey smiled as Bertie hurried outside to look.

The kids followed, with Beau and Jolie peeking around every plant to try to find the turtles. Casey knew their favorite hiding places, and he wasn't saying. The kids seemed to be having fun playing hide-and-seek with them.

"Stay on the paths," Bertie told them. "We don't want to accidentally hurt the turtles or the plants. So you can look, but no running through the plants." He bent down and pointed. "Look there. Do you see it?"

Casey smiled. It seemed Bertie had eagle eyes and had spotted Cleopatra. She moved until she was hiding under one of the large blue hosta leaves.

Casey loved that Bertie and the kids seemed to be enjoying themselves. He put up the umbrella and went back inside to put the hot dogs in to heat up. He got condiments on a tray, as well as plates and silverware, and carried them out. Phillip volunteered to set the table so Casey could finish with the cooking and carry out the buns, chips, and fruit.

It was a simple, kid-friendly meal, but Casey also had some mustard and spicy sauces for the chicken in order to try to elevate it a little for him and Bertie. "I have some steaks that I thought I'd put on the grill once the kids have eaten," Casey told Bertie softly.

The smile he got was epic. "That's so awesome."

Casey figured that Bertie was going to get tired of chicken nuggets and hot dogs. "Let's get them fed, and I figure we can get them settled with something fun before we eat our dinner."

The kids dug into the chicken while Beau ate his hot dog with just ketchup, making a bit of a mess. He seemed to be happy, though, and ate some of the chicken as well. The back of the garden got more sun than the rest of it, so Casey had planted things to attract butterflies, and Beau hurried off as soon as he had finished eating to watch the colorful insects flutter among the flowers.

Jolie followed her brother, while Phillip asked if he could go sit in one of Casey's outdoor chairs with his iPad. Bertie gave his permission and then sat back. "It's lovely back here. So peaceful and quiet. The fence gives you privacy, so it's like there are no neighbors at all. Just this little patch of heaven."

"I'm glad you like it. Growing up I hated outside work because it felt almost like punishment. Mom and Dad made me mow the lawn and do all that kind of stuff. But once I bought my own house, I learned a lot. The orchids were something I fell into and just loved. Then I sort of taught myself how to garden. I made mistakes and ended up moving things around, but now I really love it back here. It's my own little secret garden. I come out here when I have a bad day and weed, plant, mulch, and just work with my hands, and I feel better."

"That's why I became a florist. It's a connection to nature and, for me, an outlet for creativity." Bertie grinned widely. "I arrange flowers every day and design intricate floral patterns, almost mini landscapes in a container. But this is the entire thing, and it's just lovely, especially since it's such a contained space. You used the fences and even the trees, with the way some of the plants are climbing." He seemed in a kind of awe, and it really touched Casey. Many days after work, especially after a difficult shift, he came out in the garden just to ground himself. It was like the plants and soil helped remind him of what was important and that no matter what awful things one person did to another, there was something beautiful and special in the world.

Casey sighed as he settled back in his chair. "Did you all get enough to eat?" he asked when the two youngest returned from watching the butterflies. They both nodded, and Jolie practically bounced with excitement.

"Can we go look for the turtles?" Jolie asked.

"Yes," Casey answered. "But don't touch them or pick them up if you find them. This is their home, and they need to feel welcome here. Okay? And stay on the paths." Casey stood and lit the grill. Then he got the steaks going, along with some vegetables.

"You don't have to do all this. I can eat what the kids do," Bertie said as his stomach rumbled.

"I've had enough chicken nuggets to last me a lifetime. I didn't really think that steak and grilled vegetables would be something the kids would eat, and it wasn't that much work to make what they like." He turned the meat and the vegetables, closed the grill lid, and hurried inside to get a platter. When he returned, he checked everything and closed the lid once more, then got out a couple of drinks from the small refrigerator under the tiled work surface he'd built next to the grill. It was an outdoor kitchen of sorts and meant he could have things handy when he was out in the yard.

Once the food was done, he took the platter to the table and turned off the grill. All three kids seemed to gravitate to the table, with Beau climbing onto Bertie's lap. Jolie seemed more interested in watching for the turtles. Bertie offered Beau a few bites of his steak and vegetables. He ate a bit and then fell asleep in Bertie's arms.

"Would you like a little, Phillip?" Casey asked, and he came over. Casey cut him some steak from his plate, and Phillip sat and ate, a boy already starting to grow, with a nearly endless appetite.

"I found Anthony," Jolie called as though she had won the turtle lottery. "He's really pretty and has orange on him."

"That's how you can tell them apart. Anthony is the prettier of the two," Casey told her.

"Why?" she asked as she sat at the table. She ate a bite of what Bertie offered her but wasn't really that interested in food.

"Because with animals, the boy has to attract the girls, so they're usually the showier of the two. Like the turtles. He's prettier. Did you ever go to feed the ducks?" She nodded. "The boy ducks are bigger, and they're the ones with the colors on their wings. The girls don't have that."

Jolie smiled. "That's because the girls get to be fussy and can pick the best one." She had her best girl-power stance and was adorable as hell.

"That's right. Have you seen a peacock with the huge tail feathers?" Casey asked. "Only the boys have that so they can attract the girls." He gave her a light squeeze, and she gave him a smile before taking off again to where she might find Cleopatra.

All three kids were amazing, and they each had their own personalities. Phillip was quiet and loved his video games. Jolie was smart and filled with energy and curiosity. Beau loved his cuddles and needed the most reassurance. And all of them were pretty wonderful.

"This is so good. Thank you," Bertie said as he finished the last of his steak.

Phillip had eaten all of his meat and vegetables. Casey had expected him to go play his games, but he sat across from him, watching Casey intensely. "Do you really think you'll be able to find Mom? I read on the internet that people who go missing and aren't found quickly may never be found." He swallowed, his expression heartbreakingly serious.

"I'm going to do everything I can." Honesty was the best course in something like this. "I wish I could give you a definite answer, but I'll do my best." Damn, he wanted to tell him what he really wanted to hear, but that wasn't right. Still, Phillip nodded but didn't say any more, and eventually he left the table to sit in one of the other chairs to play his games.

"I know you want to have the answers," Bertie said. "But I appreciate your honesty with them."

"It's all I can do." Jenn's disappearance was troubling. Somehow she had left very little of a trail, and with every day that went by where she didn't surface to try to help her kids, it raised Casey's concerns about foul play. Something had most definitely happened—Bertie's sister hadn't just walked away from her kids. His gut told him something else was going on here, but he didn't know what. "Tomorrow I'll be able to check out her car, and maybe that will tell us some more." Something sure as hell had to, because right now, they had crap.

Beau woke up and squirmed to get down. Bertie set him on his feet, and he took off to play with his sister. "I still can't believe that we met again. It's under some of the worst circumstances, and yet here we are." Bertie swallowed hard, Casey watching his elegant throat work. "But I like to think that the world is largely in some sort of balance. We have to take the bad with the good, and…." He seemed to be searching for the right words.

"And sometimes the bad can bring the good with it," Casey whispered, because that was definitely true. Bertie's sister's disappearance was bad and heartbreaking, especially when seen through the longing and hurt in her children's eyes. Yet that bad situation had brought Bertie back into his life. "Do you ever regret what happened?" He certainly did, and many times he wished he could go back and change his decision to leave.

"Yes," Bertie answered. "But we were so young. There are stories of high school sweethearts being together all their lives, and I know it happens, but I also think we both needed to grow up." He drank his water, the ice clinking in the glass. "You went into the Navy because you must have needed something you weren't getting. And even if you didn't particularly like it, the experience helped you grow up and figure out what you did want."

"That's true. After that, I went to the academy and was able to focus on my training in a way I couldn't have before the Navy." He had always been so scattered and disorganized. The Navy helped him, with their rules and specific ways of doing things. There was no room for his disorganization. That might have been part of what he hadn't liked. Initially the experiences and rules went against his natural order—or disorder—but he changed, and because of that, he was a good trooper. "And I was such a baby when I first went to school."

Bertie chuckled. "We both were. A lot has changed since back then, and no matter how much I may have had a crush on you then, we were too different and didn't know what we wanted."

"You don't seem all that different. You always knew you were an artist. You just needed to find your medium." Casey smiled. That had always been plain to him.

"I wish I'd known that back then. I felt so untethered and was always looking for something. I just didn't know what." He sighed, his gaze growing gentle and warm. "I know myself a lot better now."

"Me too." Casey quirked a grin. "I'm well aware that I can be an ass."

Bertie rolled his eyes. "Tell me something I don't know."

Casey chuckled. "You always had a smart mouth."

"Yeah, I did." He leaned over the table, lowering his voice. "And now I really know how to use it." The way his eyes danced and then grew serious sent a wave of heat through Casey. There was nothing he could do about it, which only added to the flirty moment. Damn, Bertie was something else, and his sense of humor had most definitely deepened. In college around the lunch table, they had joked along with their group of friends, but looking back, Casey could see how they'd both kept to themselves. Casey knew he hadn't been completely comfortable with who he was, and Bertie probably hadn't been either.

Bertie seemed to have blossomed into the person he was now. Artistic, with incredible eyes and excitement that shone through, especially out here in the garden. Casey had changed as well, but he had gone another way. He'd had to find his own strength and had used it to bolster his defenses against those who might fight him. His attitude might have changed since that semester years ago, but the fear and that feeling that he didn't fit had had an effect on him. If he didn't fit, he used his strength to make it work. Bertie seemed to adapt and use his incredible personality and warm heart to win people over. Lord knows he seemed to have already gotten around the walls that Casey usually kept well fortified. Still, this was Bertie, the one man he wished things had been different with, so maybe that shouldn't surprise him.

Casey grinned. "I don't doubt that," he said softly. "Neither one of us is a kid anymore."

"No." Bertie seemed to check on the children, who were once again in the back of the yard, watching the butterflies. "We aren't, and we've figured out that life will throw us curves." He lightly touched Casey's hand. "But Casey, I'm not sure what it is you expect from me. If things had been different, you and I might have been able to see how things could be now. But I have three kids that I have to see through all this uncertainty." He lowered his voice to a whisper. "What if Jenn is never found? Or what if the worst has already happened and…?" He swallowed. "I can't say it. But we both know that my life isn't going to be the same after this. Even if Jenn comes back, there are going to be a lot of questions, and she isn't going to be able to step right back into her life and pick up where things left off. Not after this amount of time and what these sweethearts have been through." He squeezed Casey's fingers. "I have to see this through until the end."

Casey nodded. "It's possible that things will work out." Though with each passing day that seemed less and less likely. "Do you think I'm so shallow that I would turn my back on you because of them?" He realized that maybe he didn't want to know the answer to that question. Casey gently tugged his hand away and gathered up the dishes, taking what he could carry into the house, because he needed a few minutes to himself. He'd been told that he sometimes had shit interpersonal skills, but maybe he gave off an attitude that said just what he didn't want to.

"No, I don't," Bertie said, carrying in more dishes behind him. "But it's a lot to ask of anyone." He set them on the counter. "There are so many unknowns in my life right now that I can't expect anyone to be able to keep up with that." He leaned against the counter. "I'm not implying anything about you or your integrity. The kids like you, and that's a big deal. But they've been through a lot already." He sighed. "I really can't start anything now other than friendship. I hope you understand."

Casey put the dishes in the sink and then turned around. "No, actually, I don't understand." He drew closer, and Bertie's eyes widened. Casey held his gaze. "Things happen every day. Good, bad, and ugly. I'm not asking you to marry me, but I am asking that you don't turn away. Life changes all the time." Casey closed the distance, standing right in front of Bertie. "Do you really want to try to do this all on your own?"

"Not really. But I have to. Hopefully, when you find Jenn, we can get to the bottom of what happened and arrange for her to get the help she needs. Then maybe I can think beyond the next hour or so." He held still, and Casey saw a quiver run through him. "I can't do this. I can't be this close to you and not want things that I shouldn't be allowing myself to think about. These kids are missing their mom, and I keep thinking about you, and...."

"We're going to find her," Casey said. "She's out there somewhere, and we'll find her. Wyatt didn't think that foul play was involved in her accident. Tomorrow I'll be able to look at the car and see what it can tell us." He backed away, putting more distance between him and Bertie, because being that close was too damned tempting.

"I hope so. I love those kids, and I'm grateful that I get to spend time with them and get to know them again, but the circumstances around it really suck." He sighed. "Look, if you want to be friends, I am more than up for that. But if it's all too much, I'll understand about that too. This probably isn't the best time to be starting anything. But God, knowing someone is there to support me through this...." His voice faltered. "I keep wondering if I'm doing something wrong or if I'm going to end up messing up the kids somehow. I've never had kids before. I was always the cool uncle who visited and brought presents. I was never the one to put them to bed or scold them. That was their mother's job. I got to do all the fun stuff with them, and that was three years ago."

"So you're learning who they are, and you care for them." Casey tugged Bertie into a hug. "You just need to follow your heart."

"Are you talking about with the kids or with you?"

"Both." Casey held him for a few seconds longer before stepping away. "You better go check on them. I'll get the ice cream and bring it out. I think I have a few flavors in the freezer." Nothing made him feel better than a bowl of rich dark chocolate ice cream.

"Okay. I'd better make sure they aren't terrorizing the turtles." Bertie left through the back door, and Casey got all the ice cream fixings and carried a tray with bowls and scoops out to the patio.

"Ice cream!" he called, with Beau racing up. "I got you chocolate, and I've got strawberry too."

"Chocky," Beau said, doing a little happy dance. Bertie got him settled in a chair, and Casey scooped him some. Jolie took "pink," and Phillip got some of both. Bertie wanted chocolate, and Casey had both, then sat in one of the chairs as the shadows lengthened and the light began to fade.

"Is it good?" he asked, and Beau hummed and nodded.

"Fank you," he said gently, eating like crazy.

"Yes, thank you," Bertie said. "For the dinner and everything else. It was really nice." The kids were settled and quiet as they ate. Once Beau was done, he wanted to go look for the turtles again.

"You need to settle down." Bertie wiped off Beau's hands and lifted him onto his lap. Jolie seemed put out until Casey offered his lap, and she climbed up and settled against him.

"What else do you do out here?" Phillip asked.

"Just sit where it's quiet," Casey answered. "As it gets darker, you can see some of the stars. Because we're in town, you don't see as many, but I bet you saw a lot of them out at your house. I have a star map inside, and maybe sometime we can go out where it's darker and pick out all the constellations. There are lots of them, and they have stories that go with them. I bet I might even remember some of them." It had been quite a while since his uncle had taken him out stargazing.

His mother's brother was an amateur astronomer. He'd had a large telescope and used to let Casey look through it. They'd seen the planets together and many stars. It had been really something. But he'd passed away before Casey was out of high school. He had asked about the telescope, but no one seemed to know what had become of it. Casey always thought that his cousin took it or that it got sold, along with a bunch of other things. He wished he had it to remember his uncle by, because he used to love their time together.

"Really?" Phillip asked. "Mama said that she might get me a telescope for Christmas. I asked for one last year, but she said I was too young."

"Of course," Casey said gently. He wanted to make more definite plans, but Bertie was right, there were so many unknowns at the moment.

Beau was half asleep in Bertie's lap, and Jolie's eyes were closed. Casey caught Bertie's gaze. No words were said or needed. Bertie slowly got to his feet, holding Beau gently, guiding him in his arms without waking him. Phillip gathered his things and said a quiet good night while

Casey shifted. Jolie woke and stretched, still sleepy. He helped her get down and held her hand, slowly walking them through the house and then out to Bertie's car. Jolie went right into her car seat, and Casey got her buckled in. Phillip was in his place in the center, and Beau in his seat. Casey closed the door on his side, and Bertie did the same, the two of them sharing a glance in the glow of the streetlight over the top of the car.

Casey stepped around the back and onto the sidewalk. "I'll call you tomorrow," he said softly, "and if you need anything...."

"I know." Bertie held his gaze for a moment before getting inside and closing the car door. Casey stood in front of the house watching them leave until Bertie turned the corner. Then Casey went inside and locked the house before cleaning up the dishes from dinner. It was surprising how quickly Bertie and the kids had filled his house and garden with playfulness and life. And once he was done and heading upstairs, he sighed as he padded through the quiet house, wishing for more of that laughter and energy from just an hour ago.

CHAPTER 4

"BERTIE, YOU have a call on line one," Millie told him.

He looked up from the huge showpiece he was just finishing for a wedding tomorrow. He had made four of them for the church, and the plan was to take them to the reception after the ceremony. The wedding was a tropical paradise, and he had never used so many anthuriums, birds-of-paradise, and orchids in arrangements in his life. A dozen smaller versions had also been constructed for the tables, and all of it was going to be delivered first thing in the morning.

"Okay." He made a mental note of where he was and took the call. "This is Bertie. Can I help you?" God, he hoped it wasn't the day care.

"It's Casey." Instantly Bertie tensed, preparing himself for bad news. "We found Jenn's phone under the passenger seat of the car, but it's locked. Do you have any idea what she might use as a lock code?"

"Not really. She was always really paranoid about things like that, so I suspect it's going to be something very specific to her. Try the kids' birthdays." He rattled off the dates for each of them. "And try our address growing up—2983 or 3291."

"We will. Thanks. Also, Jenn might have been seen in Newville a couple days ago at a drugstore there. When I spoke to them, it sounded like her. She was there with two men. I'm on my way there now." He sounded excited. "I'll be in touch when I know more. Okay?"

"Please let me know." At least if she was seen, then he would know that she was alive. That was one piece of the puzzle. He thanked Casey and hung up, staring at the phone. But if it was her who was spotted, and she was in Newville, then why hadn't she come home? His mind was going in circles, and he needed it to stop.

"You okay?" Millie asked from next to him.

"I will be," he said softly. Bertie knew he had to get his head in the game, but it was so hard. A few days ago he had his work and his art, and now he had kids and a missing sister.

"Are the children okay?" she asked. "How are they dealing with all this?"

Bertie sighed. "Better than I am sometimes. Phillip is quiet, and I know he understands part of what's going on. He's scared but putting on a brave face for his brother and sister. Beau and Jolie just want their mother. When we went over to the house, Beau searched all over for her and then hid under the bed. The poor thing is scared, and he wants Jenn all the time. Jolie asks where her mama is at least ten times a day, and I don't have any answers for her." He headed back to his bench, where the huge arrangement sat, ready for him to add the last details. The problem was that his head was blank. He tried to call up what he had been doing, and nothing came.

"You hang in there and be strong," Millie told him.

Bertie was doing the very best he could. Standing next to the table, he stared at the arrangement, and finally his head kicked into gear and he was able to finish. Then he placed it in the cooler with the rest, making sure they were all tagged for delivery.

There was no time to waste, and he got started on the next set of arrangements, consulting his notes in order to determine what he had planned. Alice worked at the smaller table, filling the more standard orders that came through the website or over the phone. She was a good florist and able to do lovely arrangements that sold well. "Once you're done, do up a few to put in the cooler for the store. We've sold half a dozen already today."

"No problem," she said brightly as Bertie got himself into his next assignment.

There was a lot to do, and that made the day go quickly. Joseph came in around four to work the evening, along with Bertie's assistant manager, Kathy. They were a good team, and once he gave them the details for their shift, he took off to get the kids at day care.

He picked them up at the door and signed them out for the day.

"Do I have to go here?" Phillip asked as he climbed into the back of the car and slumped in the seat.

"Donald sent me a message today. He was able to help me get you enrolled in day camp at the Y. So you'll go there for the day, starting Monday." It seemed like they were making plans, but Phillip had to have a place to go while he was at work. Maybe Jenn could keep him going there after she got back, especially if Phillip liked it.

"Will Mr. Casey be here?" Jolie asked. She really seemed to be taken with him.

"I don't think so," Bertie answered.

"Do you like him?" she asked in a singsong way. "I saw you hugging in his kitchen." The little sneak. "Are you going to marry him?" She laughed as though the notion were really silly.

"Jolie, be nice," Phillip said seriously.

"Uncle Bertie and Casey sitting in a tree…," she began singing before a case of the giggles completely took over.

"You're such a baby," Phillip said like he was so over it.

"I'm not a baby. Beau is the baby."

Bertie pulled to a stop, thankful that there wasn't another car behind him, and turned around in the seat.

"I not a baby," Beau said, folding his arms over his chest. "You a baby."

God, suddenly Bertie understood why his mother had wanted to pull her hair out when he and Jenn were growing up. This was most definitely some sort of karmic payback.

"That's enough. No one is a baby anymore. You're all young ladies and gentlemen, and you need to act like it." Damn, he was tired, and he sure as hell hoped the three of them bought that line, because he was about ready to snap. "Now, let's go home so I can make you all something to eat." He needed food too, and maybe a good stiff drink once he had the three of them in bed. God, he could use more than one.

"Look!" Jolie called and pointed as they pulled up in front of the house. "A police car. Are they going to take Beau away for being bad?"

"I not bad," he countered and began to whimper. Bertie pulled to a stop behind the vehicle, wondering what the hell was happening now? Had they found Jenn and it was bad news? Not that anything associated with his sister in the past few days had been particularly good news.

He shut off the engine and helped Beau out of his seat. He set him down, and Beau took off toward the house. He hurried behind one of the bushes to hide. Bertie found him and held a shaking Beau in his arms as Casey got out of the car. Good news or not, at least it was him.

Dang, he looked good in that uniform, filling it out in all the right places. Bertie took a few seconds to look him over before he let reality tumble back in. Jolie hurried over, and Casey took her hand.

"What's going on?" Bertie asked, expecting some sort of earth-shattering news. Coming home to a police officer waiting in front of the house was rarely a good sign.

"Did you find Mommy?" Jolie asked.

"Not yet, sweetheart," Casey said. "But I'm really trying. I promise." He lifted her up and carried her to the front door. Bertie was sure he was waiting until the kids weren't around to tell him something, but he didn't know what.

Bertie unlocked the door, and Phillip hurried inside and upstairs. "What's going on?"

"I think day care is getting to him a little bit. They're used to being at home with Jenn, and now they're in day care. Beau and Jolie are taking to it with the other kids, but I know Phillip feels very out of place. Thankfully, starting Monday he'll go to the Y's program and can be with kids his own age."

Once they were inside, Casey set Jolie down, and she hurried off to get her doll. Beau squirmed to get down and raced off after her. "I know the younger two are asking for their mother," Casey said, and Beau nodded. "But Phillip is the oldest, so he's probably going to feel her loss most of all, and he isn't going to be the one asking for Mommy all the time. He likely feels he's supposed to be the one who looks out for his brother and sister. Phillip is an amazing kid, in some ways older than his years, and yet he's scared in a way the others aren't. They want their mom; Phillip is probably wondering what will happen if she doesn't return. There's a difference."

Beau couldn't argue with any of Casey's assessment.

Bertie found himself encircled by Casey's arms, and he gave himself over to it. "Maybe knowing something—anything—will help. I don't know."

Casey held him tighter. "We believe that Jenn is around and that it was her in Newville two days ago. We were able to get security video from a convenience store, and it looked like her, though I will say that Jenn looks awful. She's thinner than she was in the pictures you gave me, and her eyes are sunken, with dark circles and bags. From what we can tell, she tried to get medication that she can't have without a prescription and ended up buying cigarettes. The clerk who waited on her said she seemed really out of it."

Bertie groaned, but he'd known something had to be going on. Jenn wasn't going to take off without a reason. "Is she drunk? If Jenn drinks, she gets really depressive."

"I don't think so. From what I saw and the way she was acting, I'd say that there were things worse than alcohol that are driving her behavior. We won't know until we find her." Casey slowly released his breath.

"Uncle Bertie and Casey sitting in a tree…," Jolie began singing as she came down the stairs.

Bertie didn't want to back away. It was Casey who released him. "Be nice to your uncle." Casey tickled her, and she laughed loud and long. Beau came down, and Casey tickled him too until both kids were giggling like idiots. "I'll watch these two monkeys a minute," Casey told him, and Bertie gratefully went upstairs and knocked on the closed door to the room Phillip was using.

It opened, and Phillip sat back down on the side of the bed. "What do you want to ask me?" Bertie said as he sat next to him.

Phillip shrugged. "It doesn't matter. You won't tell me anyway."

"I'll answer your questions as best I can, but I don't have many answers," Bertie told him. "I can try to help, though."

"Do you really not know where Mom is?" Phillip asked. "She always said that if she disappeared, it was because someone would have put her away in a mental hospital."

Good God. Bertie stifled a groan. "I don't know where she is. But Casey says she's somewhere in the area. Someone saw her a few days ago. So Casey and the police are getting closer to finding her. That's good. But as for the rest, no, I don't have any answers."

Phillip nodded. "What will happen if they don't find her or if they decide Mom's crazy?" He was getting to the real heart of the matter.

"No matter what, you'll have a home here with me." Bertie's throat ached, and he put an arm around Phillip's shoulders. "You're my family, and I'll take care of all three of you. I want your mom to come back so you, Jolie, and Beau can be with her, but if something happens, you'll have a home here."

"But how can you say that? What if they don't let you keep us? What if Mom…?" He lowered his gaze to the floor.

"Don't worry about all that. If your mom can't keep you for any reason, I'm going to be here, and I'm not going to let anything happen to any of you. I promise." He sure as hell would fight for them. "As for your mom, I don't know what's happening with her. I haven't for a while."

"Not since the accident," Phillip said. "I know—Mom was different before then. She was nicer to all of us, and she used to do fun things. Now she sleeps a lot and is grumpy when she wakes up. Sometimes Beau gets hungry and Mom just wants to sleep, so I make him something to eat. Then Mom gets mad at me because he doesn't eat dinner. But he was hungry, and she won't help, and then I'm in trouble." Bertie held him tighter. In some ways, Phillip was more grown-up than Jenn ever was, and he probably had to be in order to make up for Jenn's issues.

"No matter what happens, I'll do my best to try to make things better," Bertie promised. He had no intention of stepping out of these kids' lives again, no matter how Jenn acted. "Things have been strained between your mom and me for the past few years, but that has nothing to do with you kids. I missed all three of you, and when we find your mom, she and I will work things out." He'd move heaven and earth to see to it that he got to see the three of them.

"But what if she can't take care of us?" Phillip asked, and Bertie wondered if this was a long-standing question that Phillip had had. He wasn't sure but didn't pry.

"Then I will. Without a doubt. Okay?" He'd do whatever the law required so that they didn't have to worry that they were loved and would be cared for. "We'll figure things out, and I'll talk to you about it too. Is that okay?" Phillip nodded, and Bertie hugged him. "Sometimes we worry about things we can't control. I wonder what happened to your mom too. But whatever happens, you don't need to worry about where you'll stay or if someone loves you. Because I do, and I always will." Damn, he hated the fact that Phillip should have these kinds of worries at ten years old. "Are there friends that you want to see? Maybe I can arrange for them to come over to spend time with you." Phillip shrugged, and Bertie wondered what Phillip's life was like. "We're going to have dinner in a little while, so come down when you're ready." He smiled and stood, leaving Phillip where he was.

Bertie was surprised when Phillip followed him downstairs to where Casey, Beau, and Jolie were watching Mickey Mouse on Disney Junior.

"Do you want to stay for dinner?" Bertie asked Casey. "It isn't going to be like last night. I picked up some pizzas at Aldi. They have good ones, and I'm going to put them in the oven." He could add another one.

"You sure?" Casey asked, and Bertie nodded.

"You might want to get changed out of your work clothes." Damn, that sounded dirty, because Bertie would have loved to be able to strip Casey out of that uniform and get a good look at—and feel, for that matter—what was underneath. "The pizza is going to take twenty minutes or so."

"Then I'll head out and be right back. Should I bring anything?" he asked.

"Ice cream," Beau chimed in.

"I have fruit for dessert. You can't have ice cream every night." Bertie realized how much he sounded like his mother and backtracked. "Maybe berries with whipped cream on top?" That seemed to make everyone happy, and Casey hurried out while Bertie got dinner into the oven and plates on the table.

"Uncle Bertie, you like him," Jolie said with a light snicker. "Mr. Casey is nice, but he's a boy. Boys are supposed to like girls." She put the plate that Bertie handed to her on the table.

"You like who you like," Bertie said. "And that's okay." He knew this was coming from his sister or school, so it didn't bother him. Jolie didn't seem to think it was a big deal, and she might just be teasing him. He was quickly finding out that she was a little mischief-maker. She liked to hide Beau's toys, probably as punishment for something Beau had done to her. But she was definitely a sneaky one. "You seem to like Mr. Casey too."

She nodded. "He's nice."

"Yes, he is." Bertie set the last plate on the table and scooped her up, flying her around the kitchen as she laughed. "And that's why I like him." The words were out of his mouth before he could stop them, and it felt good to express some small part of his complicated feelings with regard to Casey.

"Can we have a sleepover?" Jolie asked between bouts of giggles. Beau came in and wanted a turn, so Bertie flew him around the room, ending by setting him in his booster chair. "Mommy makes a tent in the living room sometimes." Beau bounced with excitement.

"How about another night. Maybe one where I don't have to work tomorrow. Okay?" He got pouty looks from both of them. "We'll do it, just not tonight." He wanted the kids to have a good time, but tearing up the living room when he was going to have to clean it up before getting the kids off to day care and himself to work did not sound like a fun idea.

The truth was that Bertie was tired. It had only been a few days with the kids, and he was already wondering how parents kept their sanity and didn't collapse into piles of goo at the end of the day. "Now you two go wash your hands and then come back so we can eat." They were good kids. Bertie was hoping that over time, things would get easier.

He shook his head. There wasn't going to be any "over time." Jenn had been spotted, and it was only a matter of time before Casey found her and they got to the bottom of what was going on. Still, he was going to miss them, and his life and home would feel empty when they were gone.

Casey came in the front door, and Bertie took the pizzas out of the oven, placed them on the stove top, and cut them. He got slices on the plates for each of the kids and called them to the table. "Is it still hot?" Beau asked.

"Yes. Give it a few minutes to cool before you try to eat it." He got a couple of slices for Casey and himself as well. The kids had cheese, but he and Casey had pepperoni and sausage. The kitchen smelled of sauce and spices. Casey helped the little ones test that their pizza was ready to eat, and then they all dug in.

"Good?" Casey asked Beau, who nodded and smiled as he ate. Jolie made nummy sounds, while Phillip ate quietly.

"When will you find Mommy?" Jolie asked Casey once she swallowed.

"I'm hoping pretty soon," he answered gently, but he didn't say anything about someone seeing her, which was a relief. Bertie was starting to wonder if she wanted to be found, and that worried him. Had she simply abandoned her kids? Bertie had to allow himself to realize that was possible. The sister he had known would never have done that. Jenn had changed after the accident, though, and maybe her personality had shifted enough that she would be willing to give up on the most important people in her life. After all, she had turned her back on her only brother over a ridiculous argument three years ago.

"Did you really know Mommy when she was small like me?" Beau asked.

Bertie smiled. "Yes. She used to have this doll she called Betsy. Your mom carried it everywhere the same way you do with your bear and Jolie does with her bunny. She loved that doll so much and used to put her to bed every night. That was how I knew she was going to be such a good mommy to the three of you." Bertie turned away. The Jenn he'd known had been caring and loving, though at times too trusting. She definitely was that way with men. As far as Bertie knew, Phillip had one father and Beau and Jolie another. He had never met Phillip's father. Jenn had said that he'd been a huge mistake. Hank Roussell was the father of the younger ones, but he'd taken off before Beau was born, leaving Jenn alone. Jenn had always said she had shit taste in men and held up Hank as proof in living color. But Bertie had never doubted her as a mother… until now.

"What else did she do?" Jolie asked, her eyes huge.

"Let me see," he mused. "Your mommy had a really good friend. Her name was Carrie. She went to school with your mom, and they were friends all through graduation." He lifted his gaze to Casey as though he had just hit on something. "When she got married, your mommy was her maid of honor, and she looked so pretty. Carrie picked simple blue dresses, and Jenn's really made her look amazing. Carrie married Kenneth Grant, and they live in Newville now." He hadn't thought about her in years, but it was possible that Carrie might be in touch with Jenn. He didn't want to get his hopes up, and questions bounded through his head, but he didn't want to ask them in front of the kids.

Casey had stopped chewing and nodded. He took down a few notes in the small pad he kept in his pocket. Then he put it away and continued eating, but Bertie could tell he was anxious.

"Go on and make your calls. It's okay," Bertie told him quietly.

Casey left the room and returned a few minutes later, smiling. "I have a number," he said and sat back down to finish the rest of his pizza. Once they kids were done, they went off to play in the small backyard while Casey leaned forward. "Why didn't you tell me about her earlier?"

"It never occurred to me until now. I don't know if they're in contact anymore, but it's possible." He sighed, feeling a little foolish. "Did you have any luck with Jenn's phone?"

Casey shook his head. "We turned it over to IT, and they'll try to get access. But at least we have a lead." He pulled out his phone, put it on speaker, and dialed the number while Bertie waited.

"Hello…?" The voice took him back.

"Carrie, it's Bertie Riley." He sighed. "I'm here with Trooper Bombaro of the state police because Jenn is missing," he said.

"Where are the kids?" she asked. "I can get right over there if you need me to." That was Carrie, instantly snapping into action.

"They're here with me, and they're safe. But she's been gone for about ten days now, and…."

Carrie gasped sharply. "I should have done something," she said. "I knew it."

Bertie turned to Casey, his hand shaking on the table. Casey held it gently.

"So you saw her?" Casey asked.

"Is this the trooper?" Carrie asked, and Casey identified himself. "She came by the house about… five days ago…." A scream that went up your spine the way only a kid's could sounded through the phone line. "So help me, you need to calm down or you're going right to bed, and I mean it." That tone was perfect. "Sorry, Caleb has decided he wants to run around the house like it's a roller rink or something."

"You got the mom tone down, though." Bertie was really coming to admire that ability.

"It's either that or you don't survive." She paused. "Let me think. Yeah, it was last Saturday. She and two men came to the door. They looked rough. She was nervous, and I asked her if she was okay. She said she was and that she needed some money for the kids."

"She'd left them alone about four days by then," Bertie explained.

"I figured it was a lie. She isn't the same person I knew. Anyway, I asked her inside and closed the door on the guys. I wasn't going to let them into my house with my kids. Jenn said she was okay and that she needed to feed the kids, so I gave her forty dollars and asked again if she was in trouble and needed help. She seemed spacey but lucid and said that everything was fine. I asked who the guys were, and she said they were friends of hers, but when I asked their names, she said she had to get back to the kids and that the guys were giving her a ride because something had happened to her car." She paused, and the phone was muffled; then she returned. Bertie figured it was more drama with the kids.

"I know you went over this a little and that you were concerned about her. But did she seem out of it? Frazzled? Did you think she might have been on something?" Casey asked, lowering his voice and speaking from close to the phone. Bertie lowered the volume in case the kids came inside.

"I don't know…." She was definitely hesitating.

"We're trying to help her, Carrie. She has us and the kids worried beyond belief," Bertie said. "You know me. We grew up together, and you're Jenn's oldest friend." His hand shook hard enough that Casey held it tighter.

"She looked like she had been through hell. Her face was blotchy."

"Probably because she isn't taking any of her meds, including the one for psoriasis," he interjected. "And that gets worse when she's under stress."

"Then she's under a lot of it, because it was bad. Her eyes were sort of lifeless, and she seemed jumpy and almost paranoid. I've never seen her like this. It's worse than the last time she went off her meds about two years ago. I got her to the doctor and helped her get back on them again that time." She sighed. "I have to check on the kids. They're quiet, which means trouble. But if you ask me, I'd say she's self-medicating somehow." She seemed concerned.

"When we find her, we'll let you know, and if she contacts you again, call the police right away and tell them to get a message to Casey Bombaro immediately. The sooner we find her, the sooner we can get her the help she needs," Casey interjected. He gave Carrie the number to call to get right to his dispatch.

"If you text to that number, we will receive it in our system. Any sort of communication will work." Casey flipped through his notes. "I'd like to stop by your house tomorrow and show you some pictures to see if they are the men who came with Jenn. We appreciate all your help." Casey thanked her, and Bertie did as well before ending the call.

"What do you think? Is she reliable?"

"Carrie? Yes. She loves Jenn. She really wants to help. I have no doubt about that. I'd take what she says as the truth, which scares me even more. Jenn and Carrie weren't angels growing up, so if she says Jenn was in bad shape, then she would definitely know, having seen my sister at her worst and best."

Casey nodded. "Her description sounded to me like she was on something."

"Alcohol sends Jenn into a bad downward spiral," Bertie said, still wondering what could be happening.

Casey patted his hand. "My gut is telling me that it's worse than that, but I don't know for sure. The only evidence I have to go on is what Carrie told us and the surveillance camera images, which I want to show to her tomorrow. Maybe with a better description I can get headway on who the men are. If Jenn has people with her consistently, then instead of looking for one person, I'm looking for three, and numbers are harder to hide than a single." Casey pulled out his notebook again and began writing.

Bertie left the table and went out back to check on the kids. Phillip had organized some sort of game with the other two, and they ran around the yard, chasing each other and laughing, Smidgen having the time of his life, happily barking up a storm. Bertie wished he could laugh right about now, but all he seemed able to do was worry about Jenn. Just because they had had a fight and hadn't spoken in a while didn't make her any less his sister… or the kids' mother.

He leaned against the doorframe, watching Jenn's kids play, wishing she were here to see it. They were so damned resilient. Yes, they missed their mother, yet they could play and run and just be kids. Bertie wished he could let go of his worries like that.

"You know things will work out one way or another," Casey said from behind him.

Bertie shook his head. "I don't see how. Either we find Jenn and get her some help so she can get her kids back, or we don't and they stay with me, or she's never able to straighten herself out and those kids stay with me. Either way they're screwed. They get to be raised by an uncle who knows nothing about kids, or a mother who might go off the deep end again."

Casey put his hands on Bertie's shoulders, the warmth easing away some of the tension. "Somehow things will work out for them."

"How?" Bertie asked.

"Because they have you." The words fell like rain. "Regardless of what happens, these kids will have someone who will love them. That's what kids need more than anything else. Yes, if things are truly bad with their mother, it's going to be painful for them, but you'll be there." Casey paused, and Bertie slowly turned around. "Unless you decide you don't want to be."

"Why would I do that?" Bertie asked.

"Then stop doubting yourself." His eyes were so gentle and filled with an earnestness that drew Bertie forward. Before he could stop himself, he kissed Casey, because how could he not? Casey smiled, his eyes darkening. "I have faith in you." And those words told him all he needed to hear. "And so do they. Why do you think they're out there playing and laughing? Because they already know that you'll be there for them. That you are their safety net." He held Bertie's gaze before leaning closer.

"Oooohhhh," Beau and Jolie called as they hurried over. Smidgen was ready to come in.

"See, I told you. They were kissing," Jolie said in a singsongy, know-it-all way.

"Don't be a baby," Phillip told her. "Grown-ups kiss sometimes. It's not a big deal." He shrugged, and Bertie got an image of him in a few years as a teenager. Lord help them all. "Come on. Do you want to play some more? Or we can go inside."

"Dora," Jolie said as Bertie opened the door. Smidgen hurried inside and checked his food bowl before drinking some water.

"I want mouse," Beau argued as he and Jolie raced inside like whoever got there first got to pick.

"How about you both settle down and you can color at the table." Dang, he was getting good at heading off a fight. Bertie got out the crayons and things, then cleared places at the table, put away what was left of the pizza, and loaded the dishwasher.

"I wanna watch TV," Beau said, tugging on his pant leg. "She says I color bad." He pooched out that lower lip.

"You color well, and we're having a quiet evening tonight." Bertie knelt down and hugged him. "Why not color me a picture, okay? I'll put it right up here on the refrigerator." He smiled, and Beau returned to the table.

"I'm good, and he'll put mine on the frigelator!" He said it as though it was the last word on the subject. Thankfully the two of them settled down and didn't fight over the coloring books.

"Tomorrow after I pick you up, we'll go to the bookstore, and you can each get some books to read." He made sure Phillip heard him.

"Mom gets books from the library because she says they're expensive," Phillip told him softly.

"Well, you can all pick out books to keep." He wanted them to have books of their own. It was important. "What do you like?"

"The Wimpy Kid books," Phillip said, and Bertie ruffled his hair.

"Then we'll go to a store I know in Enola. It's owned by a friend of mine. Cupboard Maker Books has used books that are a lot cheaper, and you can get as many as you want." He smiled. "Books are really important."

"Can I read on my iPad?"

"Of course. Go ahead and relax." He got the idea that there was more that Phillip might want to say, but he turned after a few seconds, looking toward the living room. Phillip reminded Bertie a lot of himself at that age. He read and tended to think things over a lot. Bertie still did that, to a degree. "There are times when we all need a chance to be alone and have some quiet time. The other two tend to be loud...." Phillip kept nodding. "Go ahead and be quiet for a while if you want."

Phillip hurried away, and Bertie checked on the rest of the kids before cleaning up the kitchen, wiping down the counters until Casey stopped his hand. "I got this. You sit, and I'll join you in a few." Casey stroked Bertie's back, and he sighed, letting some of the tension ease away... at least for now.

CHAPTER 5

CASEY KNOCKED on the door of Carrie's Newville home as early as he dared. The house was definitely awake, with the way young cries went up as soon as he knocked. A small face plastered itself to the window next to the door, and then it opened to a small girl about Beau's age. "Are you a real policeman?" she asked, and Casey knelt down.

"I am, and I need to talk to your mom," he said gently.

The little girl turned around. "Mommy, there's a policeman here. Were you a bad girl?"

Casey stood and about fell over as a woman of near thirty with black hair and wide, pretty eyes came to the door. "I'm Trooper Bombaro. We spoke yesterday about Jenn Riley." He tried to hold in a sigh. "And no, your mom isn't in trouble," he added a little louder for the peanut gallery behind her.

"Come on in," she said gently. "Can I get you some coffee?" Casey declined politely. "Kids, go upstairs and get ready. We're going to be leaving for the pool in an hour, and if you want to go swimming, then you have to get your things." She seemed like she knew how to get them moving. Carrie ushered Casey into the living room. "Please sit if you like. I'm going to get some coffee." She was gone for a minute, then returned and sat down in one of the chairs.

"As I said yesterday on the phone, I was wondering if you could take a look at these images. They're stills from video footage. Are these the men who were with Jenn?" He handed over the clearest images they had, and she looked at them and nodded.

"Oh yeah. That's them." She leaned over the image. "See what looks like a smudge there? That's a tattoo of a snarling bobcat on the side of the one guy's neck. If you know what it is, you can make a little of it out." Casey had to agree. "The other guy's arm, which you can't see here, was covered in ink. I remember because the kids peeked out and asked me if someone had used markers on his arms."

"Were any names mentioned?" Casey asked. "Did you see the car?"

"Truck. Red stripes and the snarling bobcat on the hood. It must be some sort of symbol for the one guy, I'd guess." She handed him back the picture.

"I don't suppose you thought to take down a license number?" he asked.

Carrie shook her head. She had already been an amazing help, and it was probably too much to hope for, but he had to ask. "Sorry. I wish I could help you more. Jenn is my oldest friend." She sipped from her large light blue mug and then set it on the table. "She has her problems, but whatever is going on isn't right. She was too edgy and seemed upset, though I wish I could tell you why. She insisted that she was fine, which only makes me think that she's really in trouble. Jenn always wanted everyone to think that things were perfect and that nothing was wrong. She was always one of those people to gloss over problems, but it got worse after the accident. You know about that, right?"

"Yes. Bertie has told me what he knows. But he hasn't seen Jenn in three years. He's said that he believes something is very wrong because of the way she left the kids."

"Well… Jenn's mothering skills go through phases. Unfortunately, though she can be very attentive on her own, when she's around other people, she tends to let them parent and basically ignores the kids. A month ago she and the kids went with us to the pool. She talked to the other mothers, drank in the shade, and paid little attention to Beau and Jolie. They were in the kiddie pool, splashing around, but other than the lifeguards, I was the one who made sure they didn't get hurt. She viewed it as a day out, and the kids were kind of on their own. I wish I could say that was unusual, but it hasn't been." She drank some more of the coffee as the kids came in, holding their suits.

"I'll get out of your way." Casey stood. "Thank you for all your help." He left the house and went out to his car, where he added notes about what he'd learned. Carrie had been able to connect more of the dots. He now knew that the men who had been at Jenn's house and in the garage were the same ones who were with her three days ago and at Carrie's. So they were staying close.

It could be that Jenn was relying on them for a ride, but having them break into the garage and steal things didn't add up in that scenario. Casey was becoming more convinced that, whether she knew it or not,

Jenn was being controlled, and who knew how long it would be before she was of no use to them and they hurt her… or worse.

Casey called in to the station, adding additional details provided by Carrie to the bulletin on the truck and on the two men from the video. Hopefully someone would see them, because Casey sure as heck would like to talk to the two of them.

"Another home robbery was just called in," the dispatcher told him, and provided Casey with the information. "How close are you?"

"Only about a mile. I'll head right over." He hurried to the address. He could only hope to get some additional information from this scene that he hadn't had before. But if it was like the others, there wasn't going to be much to find.

FRUSTRATION. THAT was the only word that fit as he left the latest crime scene, gripping the wheel tightly. What was it with these guys? They seemed to know when people weren't home, got in and out relatively quickly, and left very little behind. He was starting to wonder if the thieves were ever going to be caught, and it pissed him off. There had to be an angle that he wasn't looking at.

His phone interrupted his thoughts, and he answered Bertie's call. "Hey."

"How did it go with Carrie?" Bertie asked.

"Pretty good." He needed a chance to think. Casey had already checked out the various flea markets and resellers around town. The robbers had to be unloading what they were selling somewhere. "I have an idea. How would you and the kids like to take in some flea markets on Saturday?" If he couldn't catch the thieves, then maybe he could find the people selling the merchandise. "We could make a morning out of it."

"I can't. I have to work. The store is short-staffed, and I need to be there for part of the day. I can go in early, get everything opened and my work done, but then I'd need to be back in the evening to close up. I thought I'd take the kids in with me."

"How about you go in, do what you need to, and then we'll hit the markets? Then I'll bring you back to work, and I can watch the kids while you're working. That way they can be at your house." He could check out a few of the local markets again and then pick them up for a few farther away.

"That would be great," Bertie answered. "I'll see you tomorrow. I have a customer that I need to help. I'll see you then." He ended the call, and Casey pulled off into a turnout to use his computer to review Saturday markets so he could plan his attack.

NOTHING. THE markets near Carlisle and Newville had plenty of stuff, but definitely not the merchandise he was looking for. The thieves took a lot of electronics and easily sold portable goods. There were a few items like what had been stolen, but no one had an abundance. Unless they were spreading the stuff out across half the county, he hadn't come up with his answer.

Casey checked the time and got into his car, pulled out of the lot, and headed to the florist shop. There, Bertie was finishing up an amazing arrangement for a banquet. It was stunningly modern, almost severe in its use of color, and yet there was no way you could not look at it.

"Hey. The kids are in back. I'm going to need about ten."

Casey said hello to Millie, who was helping a customer, as well as the others in the store, before finding the kids in the back room. They were unusually quiet, and he saw why when he peered behind the desk. Beau had curled up on the floor and was sound asleep. "We got up early," Jolie said, putting her finger to her lips.

"I see that. Did you nap too?" he whispered.

Jolie shook her head. "I'm a big girl." As though that answered that question. Casey bent down and gently lifted Beau into his arms. He rested his head on his shoulder, arms around his neck, sleeping hard. Casey rocked gently until Bertie came in, pulled out his phone, and snapped a picture.

"Do you think I should send this to the guys on the force?" His smirk was totally wicked.

"Wyatt would get a kick out of it." Not that Casey minded. Most of the guys had kids. "Are you ready to go?"

"Yes. The preorders are done, and the cooler is full for counter sales today. Any walk-in needs are handled, and the store is staffed, so we're good to go." He took Jolie's hand. "Are you all ready to look at some fleas?"

"Ewww. Mommy said we couldn't get a dog because they have fleas," Jolie said.

"I was just joking. There are no real fleas. I promise," Bertie said.

"She knows," Phillip said flatly. "I think that was her way of bringing up that she'd like a dog."

"You have Smidgen," Casey said as the little dog wandered in. "Why don't you just love on him?"

Jolie broke away from Bertie and sat on the floor, gently petting Smidgen, who soaked up the attention. "Let's get ready to go. Smidge is coming with us, and he has a flea collar, so we won't need to worry." Bertie snapped the leash on him, and Smidgen fell right into place, walking next to him. It was adorable. Bertie took Jolie's hand in his other one, and they moved out.

"I can take him," Phillip offered, and Bertie handed over the leash. Smidgen walked with Phillip out to the car and climbed in after Phillip, then sat on his lap. Normally he rode in that spot, so it seemed he was intent on sitting there, person or not.

"We're going to the market outside Mechanicsburg first." Casey plugged the address into Bertie's GPS, and they were off.

"I'm hungry," Beau whined, still half asleep and sort of groggy.

"I put some snacks in the glove compartment before we left."

Casey got out a bag of Goldfish crackers, which made Beau and the others happy. It seemed that Smidgen liked them too.

At the market, Bertie parked and got all the kids and dog out of the car. It was quite a production. Beau went to Bertie, and Casey held Jolie's hand, while Phillip walked Smidgen. They made a real troop. "We'll look at each place."

"Can we get something?" Jolie asked.

"Maybe. We'll look at things first. Okay?" They started down the first aisle, with Casey checking out what each vendor had set out on tables or the grass. One booth had books and toys. Bertie took the kids there. They each got books, with Phillip smiling broadly as he carried his bag of booty in one hand, Smidgen's leash in the other.

"Looks like you scored," Casey told him.

"They had all the books I like," Phillip said, practically skipping as they continued down the way. It was good to see him happy, but Casey wasn't seeing what he had hoped for.

"How will you know?" Bertie asked.

"The last couple of places had some of the documentation for what was stolen, and it included serial numbers," he said softly. "I'm hoping to get lucky." This could all come to nothing, but he had to try. The usual methods weren't working, and it wasn't like the thieves would sit on the stuff like some sort of hoard. They had to have a way of turning it into cash so it would benefit them. Flea markets tended to be anonymous, with transactions largely in cash.

They finished the flea market and headed back to the car. Bertie drove toward the next market, stopping at a convenience store along the way to get things to drink.

The Williams Grove flea market was quite large, run by a train club. They had a big engine and full-sized train cars that they gave rides in. The market covered the inside of the huge train track oval and was filled with awnings, vans, and trucks. "Okay, guys, be sure to stay with us," Bertie said when he saw how large it was. Once again, they each took one of the smaller kids, with Phillip walking Smidgen, who seemed happy as anything, tail wagging.

They made their way up and down the first couple of rows until Jolie pulled away and raced ahead at full speed. Casey hurried after her. "Mommy!" Jolie called, and Casey sped up to catch her. They reached the end of the row, where Jolie stopped, looking each way. "Mommy," she cried and burst into tears. Casey lifted her into his arms.

"Where did you see her?" he asked. "Show me and we'll look for her."

Jolie pointed, and Casey followed her directions but didn't see anyone. Bertie caught up, and Casey explained quietly what Jolie had seen. "I think we need to split up. I'll take her, and you stay with Beau and Phillip. Go that way over there, and I'll look that way. Message immediately, but don't approach her right away if you can help it." God, he had no idea what was going on, but he didn't want to spook Jenn if they did find her.

"We'll do our best," Bertie agreed and went to the south, while Casey and Jolie went north. She gripped his hand hard as she looked from side to side. If it was possible for a little girl to be any more wired, Casey didn't see how.

"Do you see her?" Casey was relying on Jolie to identify her mother. They turned the corner, and Jolie tensed even more and then pulled away, hiding behind his legs. "What is it?" he asked, lifting her up. "Why are you scared?"

"The men. I sawed them." She pointed and then turned her face against his shoulder. Casey followed where she had been looking as a man came out of one of the booths, a snarling bobcat tattoo on his neck.

One of his suspects had just materialized in front of him. That couldn't be a coincidence. Casey turned away and stepped back.

"It's okay. I'm going to call for some help," he said quietly. He put in a call to dispatch, telling them what he had seen and where. "I need some units at the Williams Grove flea market on the train club grounds. Get here as quickly as you can," Casey added as the second suspect materialized. Both men strode out toward the parking lot. Shit, they were going to get away and he was going to lose them again. "Come on."

He walked as best he could holding Jolie, reaching Bertie's car just as the red truck with the bobcat on the hood slid by. Casey took down the license plate, along with the make and model of the truck. "Suspects are heading north toward Grantham driving a red Ford pickup truck, bobcat decal on the hood." He added the license plate.

"We have units responding," dispatch told him. Casey wished he could be part of the search, but the team would find them. Instead, he had to kids to watch out for.

"Are they gone now?"

"Yes. But I told the other police where they're going. They'll try to catch them so they don't scare you anymore." He headed back toward the market, where they met up with Bertie, Beau, and Phillip, who hadn't seen Jenn.

Casey explained who he had seen and where. "Stay here," he told Bertie, setting down Jolie. Then he got out his wallet and pulled out a twenty. "Take them to the snack bar and get them whatever they want." There was no way in hell he was going to scope out a booth of potential stolen goods with the kids nearby.

Once they were on their way, he wandered into the booth the men had come out of. A panel van had been pulled in, with a canopy behind it for shade. A couple of tables had been set up with various electronics displayed on them.

"Do you want one?" a woman asked listlessly as though she had just woken up. Her hair was scraggly, and the bags under her eyes would do Gucci proud. Her arms were thin, and she looked as though a stiff breeze would blow her over. She set an empty water bottle in the trash and pulled out another one before slowly coming over. "The TVs are really great, and we have more of them in the truck."

Casey looked over the smaller television sitting on one of the tables along with the DVD player and TiVo unit. He picked them up, looked them over, and set them down once again. Casey was pretty sure he was looking at stolen goods, but he needed to prove it, and that meant something more than just his gut. "Can I look inside?" he asked. "If not, I understand." He moved to the back of the booth and craned his neck. Eight flat-screen televisions of various sizes filled the back of the van. Two of them were in boxes that had been opened, and there was one sealed box. That was the one Casey wanted to get a look at. He had a picture on his phone of the receipt for a brand-new television that had been stolen. This one looked right.

"Sure." She drank more water and sat down in an old folding chair. The woman couldn't have been more than thirty, but she looked older and haggard. She also glanced around her multiple times as Casey looked things over. Nervous energy flowed off her, leg bouncing slightly when she sat.

Casey climbed into the truck and looked over the televisions, moving them slightly. When she wasn't looking, he snapped a few pictures of the backs and serial numbers, using his phone light as cover. "These are nice," he said.

"Yeah. The boss gets them at auctions and stuff," she said halfheartedly, like she didn't really care. Hell, she probably didn't. "Is there anything you want?" she asked after a few minutes.

Casey climbed out with a smile. "These are great. Let me tell my better half and I'll be back." He grinned and hurried out of the booth, trying to show his excitement. He turned back to the booth one last time before heading out of sight and then making a call. "Wyatt," he said as soon as it was answered, "I need a favor."

"What's going on? Enjoying your day off?" Wyatt fake gruffed.

"You know we're never truly off duty, and to prove it, I'm sending some pictures your way. In the robbery reports I filed, there are some serial numbers of a few items. Can you see if any match the pictures I just sent through to you? I'm at a flea market."

"Okay. Hold on. I'm pulling over now…. Okay. Which report? Do you remember?" Wyatt asked. "Nope, I found one." He took a few seconds. "Nope. That doesn't match any you gave me."

"Check the report I filed yesterday," Casey said as he checked his phone for the picture of the online receipt for the television. He smiled to himself as it matched the make and model of the boxed television. That was good.

"I got a match," Wyatt said just as Casey matched the unopened TV serial number to the one on the shipping receipt for the stolen one.

"Me too. This is definitely where they are selling their stolen goods."

"At least it's one place. If I were them, I'd be selling all over and going as far afield as I could," Wyatt said. "I'm going to call this in."

"Did you find the guys I reported as they left the flea market?"

Wyatt growled. "No. By the time we arrived, they had disappeared. We have an APB out statewide. If they show up anywhere, we'll get them. That truck is pretty distinctive."

"Well, I suspect they are going to park it somewhere now and use something else if they have the slightest clue that we're onto them." Casey ended the call to let Wyatt call in what he'd found. He was the one on duty, so Casey let him handle it. But he got a call not a minute later from his sergeant.

"You just can't take a day off, can you?"

"I was here with some friends and I saw the booth," he said innocently.

Sergeant Collins snorted. "Yeah, and I have oceanfront property in Ohio to sell you. What's the damned deal?"

"They had to be moving the stuff, so I've been going to flea markets, and I hit this one today. I've got a friend and his kids with me."

"Is this the friend who has those kids you found?" Collins asked. "Do you want to tell me what's going on there?"

"Bertie is an old friend. We knew each other in college…. We sort of liked each other back then, and we reconnected."

He sighed audibly. "And he just happens to be the guardian of the kids who are part of one of your missing persons cases. What the fuck is happening?" He was really pissed this time.

"I think the two cases are linked," Casey said quietly. "I saw the two men we identified from both times Jenn, our missing person, was spotted here, leaving the booth with the stolen goods. And I've matched serial numbers. The stuff in that booth is hot. We need to get people down here before—shit."

"What?"

"The woman in the booth is putting stuff back in the truck. Someone has gotten suspicious and they're packing up. We need someone over here right away."

"Two units are en route, but it's going to take about five minutes. Is there a way you can stall them?"

"Mr. Casey," Jolie said as she hurried over to him, "we got you a hot dog." She handed it to him.

Casey smiled and took a bite. "Thank you," he told her gently, watching the stall as the woman slowly set all the merchandise back in the van one item at a time. Casey ate the rest of the hot dog and stepped close to Bertie, sliding an arm around his shoulders. "That booth over there has stolen goods. The police are on the way, but I need to stall her. Please take the kids somewhere safe, and I'll meet you in a few minutes. Maybe back to the booth with the toys."

Bertie nodded. "Come on, kids. Let's go see the toys again."

"Why?" Phillip asked as Bertie bundled them off.

Once they were gone, Casey strode back to the booth. "You're packing up already?" The woman stopped what she was doing. "There are still lots of people around and stuff." He stepped under the canopy that she hadn't taken down yet.

"Did you decide what you wanted?"

"Yeah. We need a TV. The one we have is really old, and my other half agrees that it's best to get a new one. You have great prices." He smiled, and she paused what she was doing, which was exactly what Casey wanted. "Do you mind if I have a look again?" He thought about arresting her, but officially he was off duty, and that could get sticky. He climbed into the van like he did before without waiting for her answer and looked around, acting like he was trying to make up his mind.

"You need to decide. I have to pack up," the woman said, panic coloring her voice.

Casey backed out of the van and climbed down. "Will you be here next week?"

"I don't know. Maybe," she answered. She put the last of the electronics in the van and started to break down the tables as two cruisers pulled into the lot.

"I really need to go," she said.

Casey took her arm. "I don't think so," he said gruffly, holding her. "You are currently in possession of and are selling stolen goods. You aren't going anywhere until the police officers take you into custody."

"Are you a cop?" she spat.

"You better believe it, and you are so busted." He held her still until the others arrived, and then he turned her over to Wyatt and Martinson, who took her into custody. "The unopened television is definitely stolen. I investigated the robbery a few days ago. At least one other TV is stolen, and I suspect the rest are as well."

Martinson grinned. "Thanks, Casey. We'll take care of this and get her booked."

Casey approached the woman before they got her in the car.

"I'm not going to admit to anything," she snapped.

"Fine." He pulled out his phone to retrieve one of the pictures of Jenn Bertie had given him. "But have you seen her? She's the mother of three kids, and we're trying to find where she is." He showed her the picture and waited, watching as she hardened her expression. It was plain to him that she had seen Jenn, but whether she'd tell him was another matter. "Have you seen her?" he growled, pulling her out of her attitude. "Tell me, or so help me…." Casey added the hint of a threat and let her see as cold an expression as he could muster.

"Yeah, I saw her. A few days ago. She was at an old farm out north of Newville. Don't know if she's still there." The woman shook her head. "That was one messed-up chick, if you ask me."

"Where was the farm? Do you know the road?"

"What do I look like, a fucking atlas or something? It was a couple miles out of town." She stepped away, and Wyatt got her in the back of the police car.

"I'm going to need to talk to her again tomorrow," he told Wyatt.

"I figured. We'll hold her under suspicion for two or three days before we book her. That way you can talk to her before she goes to a judge. Who knows if she'll lawyer up or not. I suspect she's going to crash from whatever she's on in a few hours, and it's probably going to be a very long night for her." Wyatt nodded slowly. "I'll see if I can get anything more about the location of this farm and let you know."

"Thanks," Casey said and then went to find Bertie and the kids at the toy booth.

"Did you find Mommy?" Jolie asked. "I didn't see her again."

"Are you sure you saw her before?" Casey asked as gently as he could. Jolie thought and then shrugged, tears running down her cheeks. Casey lifted her, rocking and patting her back. "It's okay. If you say you saw her, then you did."

"I don't know," she said and put her head on his shoulder. The way she trusted him and held him was so touching.

"Are you ready to go back to Uncle Bertie's? We can have something to eat, and you can play with your toys and with Smidgen while he's at work." He watched her face, and she nodded. "You can help me make dinner too."

She leaned back, patting his face. "Okay."

Casey wanted to find Jenn so badly, if for no other reason than to ask her what the hell she was thinking, leaving these kids behind. It made him angry, and Casey had to push that aside because of the kids and Bertie. His main task was to find Jenn. Once he did, maybe they'd all get the answers they needed.

"UNCLE BERTIE'S home!" Beau called as he raced back from the front window. They had all worked to make dinner, and Beau's job was to watch for Bertie and alert them all when he pulled up. Beau raced in, leaping from foot to foot, with Smidgen dancing excitedly around his legs.

"Then go open the door and let him in. You get to bring him into the kitchen," Casey told him, and Beau hurried to the front door.

"Are you done working?" Beau asked, and Bertie grinned as Beau took his hand. "Come on." He tugged Bertie into the kitchen, where the table had been set for all of them and Casey already had the salad and fruit set out. Casey took the roast out of the oven and put it on the table.

"I see someone has hidden talents," Bertie said.

"We stopped at the store, and while I was there, my old friend Angela called from California. She's a chef at a fancy restaurant out there. I told her I wanted to cook something special for dinner. So I bought the roast, and she talked me through getting it ready and into the oven." His own belly rumbled as the decadent scent filled the kitchen. Man, he had done good if he said so himself.

"What's the big occasion?" Bertie asked. It hit Casey that Bertie didn't think it was a good enough occasion for something like this.

"Just trying to do something nice." He smiled and leaned closer.

"Are you going to kiss?" Jolie said. "We won't look. We promise." She actually closed her eyes and put her hand over Beau's. It was so cute.

Phillip shook his head. "Can we eat now? I'm really hungry."

"Yes, we can." Casey got a large knife and carved the roast, then gave each of the kids a small piece. Bertie cut Beau's meat up for him. Jolie insisted she could do her own, and Phillip started eating immediately. Casey got Bertie's piece cut and plated. Then he got a perfectly medium-rare piece for himself. Mashed potatoes and fruit salad completed the meal. He took his seat, paying close attention to Bertie as he took a bite of the beef.

"Oh, this is good." And damned if the soft moan didn't go right to Casey's spine and sit there, simmering away. "I haven't had anything like this in a long time." He leaned toward Beau. "Do you like it?"

"Good," he said, taking another bite. "I helped."

"Everyone did." Smidgen sat between Beau and Jolie, probably hoping for something to hit the floor. Casey had to give the pup credit. He didn't beg or bark—he just watched each bite the kids took, hoping that would be the piece that fell. When one did, he was on it, eating the beef fast and then going back on fork watch. "And it's really good."

"We made cookies too," Beau said and got a nasty look from Jolie.

"It was supposed to be a surprise," Jolie whined. "He always does that."

Beau pooched his lower lip out and began to tear up.

"It was still a good surprise," Bertie said gently, soothing Beau. "I really love cookies, and I bet the ones you made are really good." Damn, Bertie was so gentle and caring. Casey realized just how lucky he was. This whole situation was bad, but the fact that it had brought him and Bertie back into each other's lives…. He didn't want to say it was worth it, because nothing made up for the hurt these kids were going through. But there was always a silver lining, and Bertie was that for him.

He had missed someone like him in his life. Someone who cared and brought out a softer side. Casey tried to think of the last time he had cooked for someone, other than grilling, and couldn't. Here he had spent much of the afternoon on dinner, with the kids, because he wanted to do something special for Bertie.

Just then Bertie raised his gaze and caught Casey's. It was like all the air had been sucked out of the room. He knew Bertie understood what dinner meant, and under the table, Bertie found his hand and squeezed it, smiling just enough and with a gleam in his eye that Casey knew was for him. The kids might have seen it, but that expression was only for him, and it had Casey's heart beating faster and sweat breaking out on the back of his neck. He was a cop, for God's sake. A hard, seen-everything kind of officer, and yet a single smile from this man cut through all of his defenses and made him see what was possible. Casey had walled himself off because he was afraid to let his heart get involved. It had been abused before. Most importantly, Casey was coming to realize that it wasn't made of glass, and yeah, it might get broken or stomped flat, but it would heal, and it was still capable of making him happy.

"Mr. Casey? Why do you look like that?" Jolie asked. Sometimes that kid was way too observant.

"How was I looking?"

She smiled. "Soft and squishy." Jolie finished eating her dinner as though she hadn't just said something completely profound.

Bertie chuckled. "I don't think there's anything soft or squishy on Casey." The meaning went right to Casey's groin, and Casey was happy he was seated at a table.

"Yeah. He's huge," Phillip said, as though Jolie were being dumb.

She set down her fork and put her hands on her hips. "I meant on the inside. He was being soft and squishy on the inside." She rolled her eyes right back and then returned to eating, the queen having made her pronouncement. That was the end of it as far as she was concerned. So there.

Casey tried not to chuckle; he really did. In the end he mostly managed to turn it into a smile and leave it at that.

"Are you done?" Bertie asked Beau when he stopped eating.

"No. Is good. Mine." He went back to his dinner like he was starving and ate quickly, the table growing quieter as they got down to the business of food. All three kids had healthy appetites, and Casey got them more of anything they wanted.

"Can I go out back?" Phillip asked after taking his plate to the sink. Casey nodded his answer. "Come on, Smidgen," he said, and the dog looked at the table and then at Phillip. Smidgen trotted over to him, and they went out through the back door.

"I have never known that dog to step away from the table before," Bertie commented. "I think Smidge likes him more than me." His lips curved upward as he said it.

"Can I go out too?" Beau asked.

"Two more bites," Bertie said, and Beau took them before Bertie let him up from the table.

"Don't eat the cookies," Beau cautioned, and then he was gone. "Phillip, I coming to play too!"

Jolie ate the last of her dinner and joined the others.

It would be so easy for Casey to believe that they were some sort of unconventional family. The kids happily playing out back with the dog, he and Bertie inside doing the dishes and cleaning up. Casey knew that was only a fantasy. The kids weren't his and Bertie's. Hell, there wasn't a "him and Bertie." They were… well, he wasn't sure what they were, but whatever it was, this thing between them was too new for either of them to put a name to it. Still, there was no harm in a little fantasy, especially since he was coming to understand what he wanted. Not that he had a right to.

A light touch on his hand pulled him out of his thoughts. "That was a lovely dinner. Thank you."

"You're welcome," Casey said softly, turning his hand over, and Bertie slid his into it just as easy as anything. "The kids really wanted to do something, and I figured after another afternoon of coloring, they'd probably explode. So they all helped me make the dinner and stuff." He leaned closer, as if sharing a secret. "It took longer with their 'help' than it would have otherwise, but it was so much fun. Little Jolie is either going to grow up to be a chef or the head of the Army, because she loves to give orders and be in charge. Phillip is so smart and quiet."

"He's hurting and trying his best not to let it show. Phillip wonders where his mother is every second, and he's got so many questions that there aren't answers to." Bertie sighed softly.

"Beau is just a bundle of energy and joy right now."

Bertie nodded, but neither of them said a thing about the elephant in the room. It was almost like the spirit of Bertie's sister, who Casey had never met, hung in the damned air. She had been gone for more than ten days now. There was little doubt that, either through her own decisions or those of others, Jenn had for all practical purposes abandoned her children.

"I know," Bertie said softly. "I know. I'm thinking that I need to contact Donald and find out what the next steps are." He pulled his hand away and stood, then wandered over to the windows. "She's had ample time to come back on her own. As much as I want to think she'd never abandon her kids willingly, I keep wondering why she didn't come here. Why go to Carrie for money and then disappear again? I don't understand it."

"I know," he agreed. "I suggest on Monday that you call him and let him know what you want to do. You have the kids on an emergency basis, but you're going to need more authority than that, and Donald should be able to help you."

"Like a foster care situation?" Bertie asked.

"Yes. You're going to need to see what he suggests and then get some legal authority behind you. It's for the benefit of the kids."

"Okay. I will." He didn't turn away from the window. "They're so happy now, laughing and playing. That's how they should always be." He slowly faced back toward Casey. "No kid should have to wonder

where their mother is for days on end. They should be carefree. Not…
whatever this is." He lowered his gaze, and when he raised it again, his
eyes were filled with determination. "Excuse me a minute."

"Are you okay?"

He nodded. "I'm going to send a note to Donald now, asking for his
advice and help. I know he probably isn't going to answer until Monday,
but at least I'll have gotten the ball rolling." He sighed. "Even if Jenn
were to show up, it isn't like she could just walk back in and step back
into her parenting shoes. She's been gone for ten days and left her kids
on their own for nearly a week."

"Yes. She will face charges," Casey agreed. "I don't think there's
any way around that at this point. We'd be forced to file them even if
Child Services didn't." That was a certainty. "It's best to get your ducks
in a row so the kids are protected."

Bertie left the room, and Casey began clearing the table. After a
while, Bertie returned with a smile.

"Donald answered me right away. Apparently he already had things
started, and as long as I agreed, was prepared to request that I be given
guardianship for the kids pending the outcome of the investigation. I told
him that I absolutely agreed, and he's going to move forward." Bertie
started loading the dishwasher. "I don't know exactly what that means,
but I'll do whatever I have to. I don't want the kids going to live with
strangers."

"Of course you don't." Casey put aside the plate he was holding
and wound his arms around Bertie's waist. "You're doing the right thing.
I know this situation has you conflicted because you want to think the
best of your sister, but the kids are what's important, and they're danged
lucky to have someone like you." He leaned closer, pressing his nose to
the base of Bertie's neck. "You have one of the biggest hearts of anyone
I have ever met." And damn, who would have thought that kindness and
caring could be such a blatant turn-on? The longer he stood with Bertie
in his arms, the more he wanted…. Damn, he should not be having those
thoughts with the kids just outside, but he couldn't help it. "You were
always a special person, and I see now just how amazing that makes you."

Bertie slowly turned in his arms. "You don't think it makes me
selfish that after all this I sometimes wonder if Jenn will ever return? And
that I would love to raise these kids? That I think I can do a better job of
it than she can, even though she's their mother?"

Casey swallowed hard. "Wanting what's best for them does not make you a bad person. It makes you a pretty amazing one. Do you have any idea how many people in your position would turn away and let the kids go into foster care? Or would take the kids and do a half-assed job of it because they really didn't want them? I've seen it all. I know what's possible. And you loving them is not wrong." He paused and met Bertie's gaze. "At this point, unless Jenn has been kidnapped or is being held against her will, she's going to have to demonstrate that she should have her children back in her custody. She's basically abandoned them, in the eyes of the law. So you standing up for them and giving them the love they need is in no way wrong."

"But…."

Casey leaned close enough to feel Bertie's breath on his lips. "If the roles were reversed, I'd feel the same way you do." He closed the distance between them, taking Bertie into his arms, kissing him hard, holding him tighter the longer the kiss lasted. He did not want to let him go.

"Casey… I…." Bertie's eyes grew dark, flecks of green swimming in them. "The kids could come in at any time…."

"I know. But I couldn't resist." His legs shook with the energy and desire that raced through him. Casey swallowed hard, not pulling back. "I've wanted this… you… since we were in college together." He waited for Bertie's reaction to his confession.

"I'm not sure what to say," Bertie whispered, shivering in his arms until Casey realized Bertie was as excited as he was. The room wasn't cool, and energy was rolling off Bertie. "We were so young then. How could we know what we really wanted?"

"Does it matter? We aren't those people any longer. It's what we want now that counts." Casey rubbed the pad of his thumb over Bertie's cheek. "I've had years to grow up, and I've seen some of the worst of what people can do to one another. Yet in the past week, I've seen some of the best in anyone I've ever met… and it's you." He blinked and slowly released the air from his lungs. "I've made mistakes, taken the wrong path, and regretted it. When I became a trooper, I thought I was on the right path for the first time in my life. And I know I am now… because I'm right here… with you… where I should be." The words came out rough and hard because they weren't easy to find. He always thought saying what was in your heart should be easy, but it wasn't. It was fucking hard, because once said, once those words were put out into the world, they couldn't be taken back. Letting go of those feelings put them in the hands of someone else. It gave them power over you, with the ability to hurt.

The corners of Bertie's mouth turned upward. "No, I don't suppose it matters. Today is what counts. And unlike when I was in college, I have three kids who are depending on me."

Casey nodded. "I get it." He began pulling away.

"But I couldn't have done this without you. Knowing you were here to support me was... well, it takes my breath away. You made me dinner and took care of me so I'd have the energy to take care of them." Bertie moved right back into Casey's arms, resting his head on Casey's shoulder. "I don't know what's going to happen, and frankly, right now, I'm so tired I can hardly see straight." He rested against him. Casey was more than happy to support him for a while.

"Uncle Bertie, can we have the cookies now?" Phillip asked quietly. Casey could see him taking in how the two of them stood together. Then he shrugged. "You might want to move apart, or else the other two are going to sing more kissing songs." He moved right on past, with Smidgen following behind like Phillip had bacon in his pocket.

"Go get your brother and sister. Tell them that it's time for a snack. Then they'll need to get ready for bed."

Phillip went out again, and Bertie seemed to relax a little. "Is it wrong that I breathe a sigh of relief every time I have all three kids in bed and I get to sit in a quiet house and wonder how I made it through another whole day?"

Casey chuckled. "I'm willing to bet that more than anything else, that makes you a parent." The idea of the kids in bed and the two of them alone was very appealing, and he drew Bertie closer to let him feel just how much.

Bertie sighed. "But what if I mess up completely?"

"As long as the kids are happy, healthy, and well looked after, that's all anyone can hope for. Anyone can be a parent. I hate to say it, but look at your sister if you don't believe me." He caught Bertie's gaze. "Just relax and enjoy the time you have with them."

"Cookies!" Beau called as he practically galloped into the room, with Smidgen bouncing along behind.

"Okay. Do you want milk?"

"Can we have Sprite?" Jolie asked.

Bertie got out the two-liter bottle and poured small glasses for the younger two. Phillip got his own glass while Casey put the plate of chocolate chip cookies on the table.

"I made that cookie," Beau said, pointing to one that was only half there.

"It looks retarded," Jolie said.

Bertie touched her arm as she reached toward the plate. "That's not a nice thing to say. It's mean to your brother, and that is a word we don't use." Bertie was firm, but he didn't yell.

Jolie's lower lip quivered, and she was about to burst into tears. "I want Mommy," she whimpered.

Bertie lifted her into his arms. "That may be so, but we still don't talk that way." Dang, he was good. Casey figured that Jolie was using Mommy as an attempt at distraction, but Bertie wasn't buying it. "You can say you're sorry to Beau and have a cookie, or you can go up and get ready for bed."

"But I want—"

"Those are your choices." Bertie didn't back down.

"I'm sorry," she said to Beau, and Bertie put her back in her seat. She took a cookie and began eating it.

"Once you're done with your snack, you can all get ready for bed." Bertie sounded worn out.

"But I'm not tired," Beau said.

"You've had a big day, and tomorrow the store is closed, so I'll be with you all day. We can do things together."

Phillip finished his glass of Sprite and said that he was going to his room to read. Smidgen followed when he left the kitchen. Bertie sighed and got the other two up and moving upstairs. Casey cleaned up the table and kitchen, put everything away, and looked through the cupboards until he found a sealable container for the rest of the cookies.

"Are they all in bed?" Casey asked.

"God, yes. Phillip is up there reading to Smidgen, who seems to hang on every word." Bertie took his hand and led him into the living room. "He's so quiet that it worries me."

"He's the one who understands the ramifications of all this the most, though even he doesn't really get it. All he knows is that his mother is gone and that she left them behind. He doesn't know what to make of it, but it hurts. It has to."

Casey leaned back, getting comfortable on the sofa, with Bertie leaning against him.

"It's quiet, and the kids are in bed. Do you think we could talk about something else? How are things at work, other than trying to find my sister?"

Casey chuckled. "Yesterday we were called in to help with a disturbance up in Perry County that they had at the courthouse there. A prisoner tried to take advantage of what he thought was an opportunity. They called for help, but it wasn't needed. The sheriff and her deputies had it well in hand. And I've been trying to solve these robberies. The closer I get to Jenn, the closer I seem to be getting to the robbers. Both things are linked. Of course I've had other things, including a few domestic disputes. Those are always the worst, because we get called, and more times than not, the wife won't press charges. The worst thing is that we know we'll get called out again."

"I suppose," Bertie said, "there have to be frustrating things. I love my job, but there are times when I wonder what I was thinking. I really love working with flowers and gardening. It brings me a lot of joy. But the other things around it sometimes drive me crazy. The people at the store are really good at what they do, and they love the business as well."

"Then what's the problem?" Casey asked.

"The owners. They started out with the same passion as the rest of us. But in the last few years, they've come to see the place as a source of money and little more. When sales are down, they start getting on me, and when things are going well, they want more. It's discouraging."

Casey snuggled Bertie closer. "Then why don't you start your own place? You have the talent, and people would definitely come to you."

"Yeah, but I don't have the money. I bought this house a few years ago and was just able to afford it. I've worked on it so much and put all my money into it. I've tried to save, but I needed a new air conditioner, and that took a lot of what I'd saved up. It takes quite a bit of cash to get the equipment and the supplies for a florist shop. Let alone what I'd need for rent and all the basic startup costs. I used to dream of having my own place."

"Then figure it out. You were always driven. Do you do work on the side?" Casey asked.

"I have from time to time. The problem is that I can't get those flowers through the shop. I have a supplier who will sell directly to me, but only because they hate the owners and refuse to deal with them." He chuckled softly. "I need to be patient and keep working toward my goal."

"Do you think the owners would ever sell the shop?"

Bertie hummed softly. "If they thought they could get enough out of it, I suppose. But they have a son who runs the store in Camp Hill. It's bigger than mine. His store isn't as successful because that one doesn't have a designer of my caliber. They know that part of the business here in Carlisle is because of me." He put his head against Casey's shoulder. "I'm just tired, and I have a whole day tomorrow where I don't have to go in to work. The store is blessedly closed, and I don't want to even think about it until Monday."

Casey couldn't blame him at all. He figured that in addition to rest, Bertie could use some distraction… and that he could provide.

CHAPTER 6

"CASEY," BERTIE hummed as he was pressed back against the cushions, his firm lips sending waves of desire running through him. Pulling back, Casey held his gaze.

"Do you want me to go? Are you too tired?"

Bertie shook his head. "The kids are upstairs, and we're making out like teenagers on the sofa. Any of them could come looking for me, and, well… I don't want them to see me sucking face."

Casey grinned. "You mean you don't want Jolie teasing you. 'Bertie and Casey sitting in a tree…,'" he started, and Bertie lightly slapped his shoulder.

"Don't you dare encourage her," he retorted. "She's a sweet girl, but the kids have enough to deal with right now."

Casey backed away. "Then maybe I should go so you can get some rest."

Bertie slipped his arms around Casey's neck. "Or maybe we should go upstairs where I can check on the kids and then meet you in my bedroom." He drew closer, kissing Casey hard, his entire being quickly overwhelmed. If he thought about this too much and what could happen, it would only ruin things. Bertie needed to just go with it. Things between him and Casey hadn't worked out before. Maybe they weren't destined to this time. A guy taking care of three kids didn't make for the most exciting prospect for most guys. Yet Casey quivered at his suggestion, bounding upward like a jack-in-the-box. Bertie stood, turned out the lights, and took Casey's hand to lead him up the stairs.

Bertie stopped at the room Phillip was using, and Casey went on, his fingers slipping away. Bertie missed the touch. He thought about it for a few seconds before sliding the door open a little more. Smidgen lifted his head from the foot of the bed and then lowered it again. Phillip was sound asleep with the dog pressed to his leg. "Good boy," Bertie whispered softly enough for Smidgen to hear. Then he backed out, leaving the door cracked open.

He then found the other two sound asleep, each holding their stuffed toy. They were so sweet, and all Bertie could do was shake his head and wonder what Jenn could possibly have been thinking… or not thinking… to have let go of these kids for any reason.

He wiped his eyes on the back of his hand and closed the door partway. Then he went to his own room, where Casey lay on the bed in only a pair of boxers. For a moment, Bertie forgot how to breathe.

Casey was all lean muscle. Bertie raked his gaze over him. Days of wondering what was under those clothes, and now in the silence he had his answers, words failing him, because damn… just damn. Powerful legs, narrow hips, and strong chest, all capped with intense cobalt eyes and a wry smile that sent Bertie's body into overdrive. Casey said nothing, just lifted his arm and took Bertie's hand, tugging him closer.

"Did you always look like this?" Bertie asked. "Because hell, if I'd known, I'd have jumped your bones back in college. Even my imagination wasn't this damned good."

Casey rolled onto his side and then sat on the edge of the bed, tugging Bertie's shirt off over his head. What Casey did with it, Bertie didn't care, his entire being focused on where the back of Casey's hand rubbed against him. "Get your shoes off," Casey whispered, because Bertie just stood still. Finally the words registered in his mind, and he got them off. Casey opened his belt and then his pants, and slipped them down his hips. Once they pooled around his ankles, Casey tugged Bertie onto the bed, manhandling him until Bertie's head rested on the pillows.

"Going caveman on me?" Bertie asked.

"You just seemed a little short-circuited," Casey told him, and Bertie had to agree, though no one would blame him for a second.

"With all this hotness to look at, I think I'm entitled." Bertie decided to let his hands do the seeing, running them down Casey's hip and then over his fabric-clad butt, squeezing slightly. Casey kissed him again, and Bertie went with it, giving himself over to Casey. He had dreamed of this for so long, and now it was almost hard to believe the two of them were actually together like this. Casey had been his imagination's go-to image for years, and now to have the man in bed with him was almost too much.

"Just relax," Casey told him.

"How can I? You're like a furnace, and I feel like I'm going to explode at any second. Just being here like this is enough that it's going to be all over damned fast if I'm not careful." He so didn't want that to happen. Bertie breathed deeply, his hands on Casey's firm strong chest, their gazes meeting, and just like that, he grew calm. This was Casey. He knew him and had for a long time. Drawing closer, he kissed him, tugging Casey down on top of him, relishing in his heat and weight pressing on him.

"You're beautiful, Bertie," Casey whispered. "What's the eye-rolly thing for?"

"Come on. Guys want to be hot and sexy, maybe handsome or rugged like you. Beautiful, though?"

Casey rolled his fingers through Bertie's hair. "But you are beautiful. Your eyes are so intense, and those lips of yours... I want to kiss them forever. You taste like summer rain and warm breezes."

Bertie thought about calling Casey out for his cheesy line, but before he could, Casey kissed him again, and Bertie didn't care if it was a line or not. Heat rose as Casey slipped off Bertie's briefs, then his own boxers. They were skin to skin, heat sliding against hard, intense heat. Casey watched him so closely, it made Bertie feel almost cherished, and that was a completely new sensation to him.

"Hey, where did you go?" Casey asked as Bertie's attention returned.

"Sorry. I got lost in my own thoughts for a second," Bertie said, cupping Casey's cheeks in his hands.

"Then I'm not doing things very well, am I?" Casey asked.

Bertie smiled. "I'm sorry," he whispered as Casey shimmied his hips. Bertie inhaled sharply, and all thoughts of anything other than Casey zipped out of his mind. Damn, Casey was hot as hell, and he made Bertie feel like he was the center of the universe. Casey rocked slowly, kissing hard, and Bertie lost himself, flying, with Casey pushing him higher until all he could do was hold on until his control snapped.

Bertie tumbled into sweet oblivion, with Casey following right behind, the two of them clinging to each other as they slowly returned to reality. He could hardly breathe, and he held still, letting the pleasant warmth of afterglow wash over him. Fatigue caught up with him after a few minutes, and Bertie closed his eyes, holding Casey and just letting himself be.

He didn't register much of anything until Casey slipped out of the bed. He returned with a towel that they used to clean themselves. Bertie curled around Casey when he returned to bed, and slid his hand over Casey's strong chest as exhaustion claimed him.

BANGING... SOMETHING intruded on the most amazing dream he'd had in years. The banging came again, and Bertie blinked open his eyes, wondering what was going on. The banging sounded once again, and he realized the sound was real and that someone was at the front door.

Bertie untangled himself from Casey, who snuffled and rolled over. "What's going on?" Casey mumbled.

"Don't know." Bertie turned on the light next to the bed and stumbled to his closet. He grabbed his robe, pulled it on, and left the room, hoping to hell that whoever was down there didn't wake the kids or he was going to kill them. At the front door, he peered out, turned on the front light, and pulled it open. "Jenn?" he asked.

She pushed inside and closed the door. "Where are my kids?" she demanded.

"Quiet," he told her. "They're all upstairs asleep, and you aren't going to wake them up."

She charged toward the stairs, but Bertie grabbed her arm and guided her through the house and back toward the kitchen, where he closed the door. "Where have you been?" She looked like hell. Her hair was stringy and lifeless, like she hadn't washed it in days. "What are you doing here at three thirty in the morning?"

"I want my kids. I have friends who gave me a ride here, and I'm taking my kids," she snapped.

"What's going on?" Casey asked as he came through the door in his jeans, barefoot and bare-chested. "You must be Jenn."

"She says she's here to take the kids," Bertie said as calmly as he could.

Damned if Casey didn't fold his arms over his chest. "I don't think so."

"They're my kids."

"Who you abandoned almost two weeks ago. They spent a week home alone with nothing to eat but peanut butter, jelly, and pickles. Right now Child Services has placed Beau, Jolie, and Phillip here. And because of your actions, it's going to take a judge to return them to your care, and that isn't going to happen at this hour."

"And who are you?" Jenn could be snarky and harsh when she didn't get what she wanted.

"A friend of your brother's and one of the state troopers who found your kids."

"I have to take them. I'm here with friends and—"

Casey narrowed his eyes. "Are those the same friends you showed up with at your friend Carrie's?" He was already heading toward the door.

"No." Her shoulders slumped. "This is Melissa. She has a car. I heard through Carrie that my kids were here, and I came to take them home."

"I'm sorry, but you can't do that. I suggest you go home and contact Child Services in the morning to let them know that you've returned. They will make an initial determination on the placement of the kids." Bertie was so glad Casey was here, because he had no idea what he should do. She was the kids' mother, after all.

"These are my kids, and you can't tell me what to do," she snapped at Casey. "I always knew you only wanted to take my kids away from me and would do it as soon as you got the chance," she added, swinging around to Bertie.

Bertie glared at her. "I kept your children from going to strangers, Jenn. You need to do what you can for them, and that doesn't mean coming here at three in the morning to try to take them away with a spurious friend. How do we know you aren't going to put them in danger? After all, the people who showed up at Carrie's are wanted for other crimes." He stepped forward. "Where are they, Jenn? Those two men? Who are they, and what are they to you?" He was determined to take control of this situation.

Jenn, as usual, began sputtering and trying to deflect, which told Bertie that he was on the right track.

"Where are they?" Casey asked. "I want names and the last time you saw them."

She grew more agitated and began stuttering a little, her eyes huge.

"I know you, Jenn. Don't try to come up with a lie to feed us. Just tell us the truth. Who were those men, and where are they now?" He was tired, and Jenn's usual roundabout way of storytelling wasn't going to cut it.

"I don't know where they are. I thought they were friends, but...." She was on the verge of tears, though Bertie knew that was only part of the show. He had seen this particular performance any number of times. One at a time, Jenn would run through the things in her bag of tricks until something worked.

"What are their names?" Casey asked levelly. "Bertie, please get my phone so I can call in one of the on-duty units. They can take her in, and then we can ask her all the questions we want from an interview room, followed by a cell as we wait for child abandonment charges." Damn, it seemed Casey knew Jenn's game too.

"Richy and Zach. They have a farm out toward Newville," she finally answered, probably realizing nothing was going to work.

"Is that where you've been?" Bertie asked, but Jenn shrugged, and it hit him that Jenn probably had no idea where she'd been or what she'd been doing. The oversized bags under her eyes, sallow skin, and unwashed hair told him Jenn had probably spent the last ten days under the influence of God knows what.

"I gotta go," she said again. "And I need to get the kids back home. So get them up and ready to go."

Bertie shook his head. "Nope. The kids stay here because they're under Child Services' jurisdiction now. I can't give them to you until they say it's okay." And there was no way in hell he was letting those kids go with her when she was half out of her mind. All Bertie could think was that Jenn had spent most of the time she'd been gone self-medicating herself into a stupor.

"I knew you just wanted to take my kids. Why do you think I never let you see them?" she yelled.

"That's enough," Casey snapped back. "The reason your kids are here is because of you, not him. You need to get your shit together if you want to get your kids back. Have your friend take you home, and we can arrange for them to talk to you tomorrow. Go home, go to bed, and for goodness' sake stay there. If you want a chance to get the kids back, then you need to clean up, stay available, and get your head in the game." Casey opened the kitchen door and escorted Jenn out front.

Bertie checked through the curtains. A car idled in front of the house, and once Jenn came out, a woman hurried around the car and helped Jenn inside. Then they took off, and Bertie wondered if he was going to see Jenn again.

"Why'd you let her go?" Bertie asked Casey. "Couldn't you have arrested her or something? At least then we'd know where she was."

"I probably could have tried, but I don't know if the charges would be strong enough to stick. Usually once the parent shows up again, Child Services takes over to see if they warrant having their children returned, which is usually the case, given the laws here. Parents are much preferred over other caregivers."

"So after all this, she turns up again and they just give her the kids? She's out of her head, and God knows what she's been taking," he said earnestly, keeping his voice as soft as he could.

"Yeah, I know. It's a frustration we have too. Arresting her wasn't going to get us anywhere. I doubt she knows very much, and I'm sure the men I'm after didn't tell her their last names. They just provided whatever it was that Jenn wanted, but who knows what she did in return."

Bertie tried not to think about it. Instead, he locked the front door and turned out the lights. He hoped that Jenn went home, slept it off, and they could try to figure things out... eventually. Right now, all that mattered was that the kids were safe and cared for. Jenn was in no position to take care of them at the moment, and who knew what she would do if she had them again.

"We'll figure all of it out in the morning," Casey told him, and Bertie followed him back upstairs. He checked on all three kids, who were still sound asleep. Thank goodness none of that racket had woken them. Even Smidgen was snoozing at the foot of Phillip's bed.

"Do you think I should send a message to Donald so he knows what was going on?"

Casey guided him toward the bedroom. "I think you need to go to bed and try to get some sleep. You can tell him in the morning. When I get up, I'll take a run out to Jenn's to try to talk to her some more. Maybe we can get a little more information."

Casey lifted the covers, and Bertie slipped into bed. Casey climbed in as well, and Bertie curled against him, happy that he had Casey to rely on. He was barely able to keep his thoughts together at the moment.

"All I want is for the kids to have a safe place to live. And I don't think Jenn is capable of taking care of them right now." He settled in bed and tried to sleep, but all he could think about was Jenn and the way she looked like hell, and he worried about his sister until he finally fell asleep.

"WHAT SHOULD we do?" Bertie asked Casey on the phone as he sat behind his desk before the store opened. "I already phoned Donald and spoke to him about what happened last night. He said that won't have any effect on what he was going to do today other than adding to his case because of her behavior."

"Jenn wasn't at the house this morning. I did update the missing person report and closed it. She has been found, as far as the law is concerned, and if she isn't at the house or where she should be, then it's up to her now. If she doesn't want to stay where she can be contacted, she doesn't have to." Jenn was an adult, and there was nothing Bertie could do about it.

"Does it make me a bad person to hope that she stays away as long as she's behaving like this?" Bertie asked quietly. "I'd like to try to help her, but I don't think Jenn wants any help."

"Your sister has spent the last two weeks as high as a kite. I'm willing to bet she doesn't even know how much time has passed. She stopped taking her meds, began feeling terrible and out of control, then probably slipped into self-medicating. I don't know what she's been using, but this isn't very good."

"If we see her again, we need to do something to get her away from these people. I didn't recognize the friend from last night. Maybe it was another person from that group." He had no idea what the hell was going on, but Jenn was definitely in trouble—he knew that deep down— and he was helpless to do anything about it. Maybe he should have had the police come and take her in. It was possible they could have gotten something coherent out of her. Though knowing his sister, it was more likely that she'd get stubborn and tell no one anything.

"She's off in her own world right now. Maybe she'll snap out of it and maybe she won't. We aren't going to know until it happens." Casey sounded as down as Bertie felt. "The thing is that she's involved somehow with these robberies that I'm investigating, so even if the missing person case is closed, I'll still keep an eye out and try to find her. I doubt she knows anything about that, but she might be able to help us find our suspects." He paused. "I need to get back to work."

"Me too. I'll see you later." Bertie hung up and sat at the desk, wondering what he would have done without Casey and knowing that he had to do all he could for Beau, Jolie, and Phillip. He knew they missed their mother, but seeing her the way she was last night would only hurt them more.

HIS WORKDAY was hectic, with orders coming in fast and furious. He and the other designers barely had a chance to breathe between customers coming in to buy arrangements from the cooler or placing special orders. Just keeping up at all was a challenge. It didn't help that the day care called because Jolie fell on the playground. She wasn't hurt, but she was inconsolable, and they called Bertie so he could try to calm her down. All the little girl wanted was her mother, and it seemed that after her brief appearance last night, Jenn had gone missing once again.

Finally, he said good night to everyone and left the store in Alice's hands before going to pick up the kids at day care and Phillip at the Y. The drama from earlier seemed forgotten, all the kids talking at once, excited and telling him about their day. "Okay, one at a time. Beau, why don't you go first?" Bertie said.

"I played trucks with Mello, and he took all the trucks away and said I couldn't play anymore because I got the red one first and he wanted it too. But I had it first, and he said I should share, but he wouldn't share his, so I kept the red one. Miss Violet said we both had to share. So I gave him the trucks and played with the Legos, and I didn't share with him either." Oh, the drama of four-year-olds.

"Cindy was really mean, and she pushed me on the playground when the teacher wasn't looking," Jolie reported. "I told her that wasn't nice and that she shouldn't push."

"Good for you," Bertie encouraged.

"Then I told her she was a dumb doodie-head."

Great. "That wasn't a good thing to do. No one likes to be called names." He bet he was going to get that little incident reported in his end-of-the-week email. "Why would Cindy like you if you call her names?"

"Because she called me names, and I don't like her anyway. The other kids don't either. She's always mean to everyone."

Bertie sighed and shook his head. "Phillip, how was your first day at the Y?"

"Cool. Thank you for getting me in there. Some of the kids I go to school with are there, and they said that I need to bring in a bathing suit for Friday because we're going to swim. But do I have to do that? I...."

"Phillip swims like a rock," Jolie pointed out. "That's what Mommy says."

Well, that explained a shit-ton about Phillip's confidence. He needed to be encouraged and not put down. "Why don't you take your suit with you and stay in the shallow end? Maybe we can go to one of the pools and help you learn to swim better." He figured he could ask Casey about it. Bertie was an okay swimmer, but he was willing to bet Casey was good at it.

"Is Casey coming over?" Phillip asked. "And is he your boyfriend now?"

"Do you not like him?" Bertie asked. He saw Phillip shake his head in the rearview mirror.

"He's nice and stuff." Phillip grew quiet again, and Bertie wondered what was going on inside his head. He drove the rest of the way home and went right inside to start heating up chicken nuggets for dinner.

The doorbell rang just as he got the kids settled at the table. "Hey, Donald," he said gently, opening the door to let him inside. "What's going on?"

Donald motioned toward the living room, and Bertie closed the door and stepped into that room. "The judge granted you temporary custody of the kids. I explained that Jenn showed up last night and the basic circumstances. Quite frankly, she was none too happy about the mother showing up at three in the morning to take the kids. It only shows a lack of concern for them. There will be a hearing in a few weeks, but until then, the kids are placed with you." Donald handed Bertie some paperwork. "This is a copy of the order. If Jenn shows up again, at least now you have a solid legal basis for keeping the kids with you."

"Casey went by the house this morning and apparently this afternoon as well, and Jenn isn't there," Bertie said. "So, she shows up in the middle of the night and then disappears again. I don't know what to make of any of it, but I do know I'm going to do whatever I can to protect them." He sighed and shook his head. "It really sucks that the person I need to keep them away from is their mother." He lowered his gaze to the floor.

Donald sat down, and Bertie did the same. "I have to ask. Are you really up for doing this? It's a huge responsibility. I know you know that. But… I have to be sure."

Bertie lifted his gaze. "Of course I am. I'll do whatever I have to for them. I'm their family and the only one they have other than Jenn." Suddenly the insecurity evaporated. There would be time for that later.

"Okay. These are things that I have to ask."

"You probably should have done that before the hearing and shit today," Bertie said sarcastically and then rolled his eyes.

There was a soft knock, and then Casey came inside. Bertie relaxed as soon as he saw him.

"What's going on?" Casey asked. "Is everything okay?" He stood beside Bertie's chair, looking fine and impressive in his trooper uniform.

"Everything is fine," Donald told Casey gently. Then he stood. "If it's okay, I'd like to see the kids for a few minutes."

Bertie stood, and Casey wrapped an arm around his waist. Then they followed Donald into the kitchen, where he sat at the table with the three kids, speaking to them softly.

"Don't worry. He won't upset them. Donald has a real way with kids," Casey said, and sure enough, Jolie and Beau grinned, and even quiet Phillip seemed to open up to him.

"Go ahead and finish your dinner."

"Thank you for getting me into the Y program," Phillip said as Donald got up. "It's great, and the kids there are really nice." Phillip actually smiled.

"You're welcome. I'm glad you're happy there," he said.

Bertie walked Donald out, thanking him for his support.

"They've been through a lot and are doing remarkably well."

"I'm trying." He opened the door. "Thank you for everything."

"Are you kidding? You've made my job so much easier, and the kids are relatively happy and settled. That makes all the difference." He paused at the bottom of the stairs. "Don't doubt yourself. Whatever you're doing, keep it up." He smiled and went out to his car.

Bertie waved and closed the door.

"Are you okay?" Casey asked. "You look worn out." He placed the back of his hand against Bertie's forehead. "You're a little warm."

"I'm fine. Just worried and tired and everything else. I barely had a chance to breathe at work, and Jenn is apparently God knows where once again." He just had too much to worry about. There was no fucking way he was going to get sick. Not now.

"I checked at the end of my shift, and the house was empty. There was no sign of Jenn, and the inside of the house is just the way we left it. So she probably hasn't been there at all."

Bertie narrowed his gaze, keeping his voice quiet. "Then what the hell is going on? She shows up at three a.m. to take the kids home, but she hasn't been there? I assumed that Carrie told her that the kids were with me… but…." He rested his head on Casey's shoulder. "What the hell is going on?" He shivered, raising his gaze to Casey's. "What the hell would have happened if we'd let her take the kids? What sort of hellhole would they all be in right now?" His imagination was taking over.

"I'm trying to work that out. I've narrowed down the area where that farm where our suspect saw Jenn could be. I'm spending every spare moment out looking in that area. But there are quite a few smaller roads and out-of-the-way places. I spoke to her again today, and I don't think she remembers a great deal." Casey held Bertie tighter, his warmth settling some of the uncertainty. "She's had a rough couple of days coming down off of whatever she was on."

"And you think Jenn is in the same boat?" Bertie asked, knowing Casey was probably right. The sister he knew was nothing like the person he'd seen last night. The Jenn he'd known was a woman who loved her kids and wanted the best for them. Not that banshee who had shown up in the middle of the night wanting to take them away with some stranger in a strange car.

"It's very possible. She looked like hell last night," Casey said. Bertie wished he could disagree, but he couldn't. Jenn had been as manic and nearly out of control as Bertie had ever seen her.

"What are we going to do?" Bertie asked.

"Well, for one thing, you're going to do what you've been doing and watch the kids. I'm going to do my best to find Jenn and this farm where she's been seen. It's possible that she's still there. Once we find her and I get the damned people she's with—because I suspect they're behind these robberies—we'll get Jenn the help she needs and hope she can get her life back on track. In the meantime, you and I will do our best to take care of her kids."

Bertie sighed. "I can't ask you to do that. You didn't sign up for any of this." This was almost too much for him to take. Bertie couldn't ask Casey to put up with all the drama that was sure to be flying around. "You're a sexy, handsome, 'get out there and do stuff' kind of guy, and for the time being at least, I'm a parent… well, of sorts, anyway." He sighed and looked into Casey's eyes. "You deserve someone who's going to be fun and able to do things." God, how his life had changed in just the matter of a week or so.

"Hey, I get what you're saying, but don't you think I deserve to make my own choices? I lived for my job. It was all I had, and I can tell you that made me a driven kind of guy."

"I know. I bet you're amazing at what you do."

Casey snorted. "What it did was make me an asshole," he whispered. "I worked shifts for the other guys because they needed it, and then I held it over them, thinking I was better than they were because I was doing them a favor." He shook his head. "What I didn't realize was how important and nice it was to have someone at home. They all knew that already, and I was clueless."

"I don't think I get what you're saying," Bertie said softly.

"All the guys knew something that I didn't. They had families to go home to and lives outside of work. Things that gave them something other than the job." Casey held him tighter. "Anyway, I thought I was better than them, and I guess that made me a real asshole a lot of the time."

"There's nothing wrong with being good at your job," Bertie said.

"No. That's just it. I wasn't any better than they were. I just thought I was. But you and the kids have given me perspective. There are things I want, and they're more than just work." Casey leaned closer and kissed him gently.

"They're kissing," Beau reported to the other kids as he ran back into the kitchen.

"Like Mommy does sometimes with her yucky boyfriend?" Jolie asked. She must have gotten some sort of answer. "Ewww."

Casey pulled away and put his hand over his mouth. He was trying not to laugh.

"Very funny," Bertie whispered. "Now go in there and use those cop skills of yours to find out about this boyfriend. What if he's one of the people you're looking for?"

Casey gasped, not laughing now. "You want me to interrogate children about their mother?"

Bertie crossed his arms over his chest. "Chicken?" He was about to make clucking noises when Casey turned toward the kitchen.

"Are you all done eating?" Casey asked.

Bertie joined them.

"Beau saw you kissing," Jolie said. Phillip had the grace to roll his eyes.

"Yeah. We heard," Casey said. "Apparently we kiss the way your mama and her boyfriend kissed."

Jolie set down her fork. "That's what Beau said. Mommy didn't know we were watching her, but we saw her kissing out by his car."

"What did he look like?" Casey asked, and Jolie shrugged. "Did you see him?"

She nodded, and Beau did too. Phillip took his plate to the sink and left the room without a word. "He was ugly," Beau said. "Really ugly."

Casey sat down with the two of them, and Bertie followed Phillip into the small living room.

"Go ahead and sit down," he said gently. "I'm not trying to get into your mom's business, but we're trying to find her."

Phillip nodded. "I know she was here last night. I heard her down here." He pursed his lips. "She was acting all weird again." He lowered his gaze to the floor, and Bertie's heart ached for him. No one should have to see their parent going off the rails. It made him wonder how much Phillip had seen and how much he'd had to deal with.

"Did you meet this boyfriend?" Bertie asked. Phillip nodded. "Is he one of the men who robbed the garage?" He shook his head. "What did you think of him?"

"Scummy. Mom used to have nice friends. But now she.... Sometimes when they came over, I told Beau and Jolie to hide from them. Mom would stay downstairs, and we'd play upstairs. They would go away after a while, and Mom would be weird for the rest of the night. In the morning she'd sleep in really late, but then she could be fun and play games with us." The things this kid had seen were more than most adults could take.

"Okay. Thank you."

"If she comes back again, will we have to go with her?" Phillip asked. That question alone was enough to chill Bertie to the bone. "I like it here. No one yells all the time, and it's quiet and we can just play, and Jolie isn't scared and Beau doesn't hide under the bed."

"No. You'll stay here until your mom is able to take care of you. I'm not going to step away or stop fighting for all of you until that happens." Bertie knew that was the most important thing he had done or could possibly do. He held out his arms, and Phillip went right into them. "I promise I'm not going to let anything happen to you. Even if I have to disappoint your mom."

"I love her," Phillip said, and Bertie held him tighter.

"I know you do, and you should. She's your mom. But right now she isn't in a good place to be able to look after you. So that's what I'm going to do." He wasn't going to badmouth Jenn in front of the kids, no matter how angry and disappointed he was with her right now. Instead, he did his best to reassure Phillip that he was going to be there. "Do you want some cookies or something?"

Phillip nodded and sat back up, wiping his eyes. "No one tells us anything. Mom doesn't most of the time. Things just happen, and I don't know why."

"Like what?" Bertie asked.

"Like there's no internet or the heat gets turned off. Last winter we were so cold for two days. Then Mom got it turned on again. After that, the internet went out and my tablet didn't work anymore." It didn't take much for Bertie to figure out what had been going on.

"I'm sorry for that. I'll try to tell you what's happening." No wonder Phillip was quiet and on edge. He was always wondering what was going to come next. Not that he could do anything about it, but he had to live with the consequences. It must be like walking around quicksand pits all the damned time, never knowing when you were going to get sucked in.

"Okay," Phillip said.

Bertie got up and gave Phillip another hug, and then they joined the others in the kitchen. Casey had gotten out the cookies, the two younger ones each munching on one. Bertie offered the container to Phillip, who took a single cookie and sat down. Bertie had one as well.

"You all can go play for a while if you want to. Then in an hour, you two munchkins need to get ready for bed."

"What about Phillip?" Jolie asked.

"He's older, so he can stay up a little later," Bertie said. "Now finish the cookies so you can go play." Bertie had new respect for his own parents. This was exhausting, and it never ended. Still, these kids deserved it.

Casey stood next to him, and Bertie sighed as he gently rubbed his shoulders. He lolled his head to one side, letting go of some of the tension he carried. Bertie knew that no matter what was to come as far as Jenn was concerned, this situation wasn't going to resolve itself quickly, and he needed to prepare himself for the next steps, no matter what they were. All he could think about at that moment was how grateful he was for Casey.

CHAPTER 7

CASEY HATED leaving the house in the morning, but he knew he had to get an early start if he was ever going to find this danged farm. Bertie mumbled in his sleep and rolled over as he got out of bed. Casey leaned over and lightly kissed him on the cheek.

"Love you...," Bertie whispered, and Casey stilled instantly. Bertie's eyes didn't open, and he snuggled down under the covers, not moving anymore. Casey figured he must have been dreaming or something, even though his pulse raced at hearing the words.

They weren't real—couldn't be. It was just Bertie talking in his sleep.

Casey dressed as quietly as he could and left the bedroom, carrying his shoes along with him. He couldn't help peeking into the kids' rooms. Smidgen lifted his head and got off the bed when he peered into Phillip's room. Together they checked on the younger two. Smidgen jumped onto their bed and settled back down, and Casey went down the stairs. He pulled on his shoes in the living room and left the house, went right to his car, and headed home.

Once inside his house, he changed into his uniform and ate a quick bite before getting into his own car, calling in to let dispatch know where he was heading.

The sun was rising behind him as he made his way out of Carlisle toward Newville. He had vague directions and had eliminated a number of places from his search area already. Taking Newville Road west, he headed most of the way to the small town before turning north. He really hoped his information was marginally correct. After some additional questioning, their suspect had given him a few landmarks, and he'd located them on satellite images, so he turned earlier than he had before. When he found the barn with three silos, he turned again and started looking.

"Is there anything unusual about the farm?" Casey had asked her for the second time. "Anything that would make it stand out?"

She had shrugged. "The house was white." Like half the farmhouses in the area—that was really helpful. "I remember it had light blue shutters, and some were falling off," she added. Getting that information had been like pulling teeth.

So he was looking for a white farmhouse with light blue shutters in poor condition. At least that was what he *thought* he was trying to find.

Once he got beyond the three-silo farm, he kept his eyes peeled for that farm he needed. He went four miles and found nothing. After making a turn north, he continued until he found the next cross street and kept looking, checking out side streets before returning to his main road and trying yet again.

He knew it was only a matter of time before he got a call and had to give up for another day, but he continued for as long as he could. This sort of work was tedious and time-consuming, but sometimes it was the only way to get the job done.

Casey figured his luck was going to run out at any time when he turned a corner toward the end of what was going to be his final pass of the day. A faded white farmhouse with a barn behind it and light blue shutters sat off to his left. He slowed slightly, looking around as he passed. There didn't seem to be anyone about, but a car and an old truck sat in the drive. Casey noted the address and called it in to the station.

What's your plan? Wyatt responded a few minutes later via message.

Casey pulled over to the side of the road. *I'm not sure. If this is the right house, I don't want to clue them in that I've found them. If it's the wrong one, I don't want to scare the owners half to death.* He could pull in and knock on the door with some bullshit reason, like a report of a rabid dog in the area and he was following up to see if they had seen it.

I'll meet you up the street, and we'll handle this together. Give me ten minutes, Wyatt messaged.

Casey agreed and turned the car around so it faced the farm, and then worked on some reports on the computer while he waited.

Wyatt pulled up behind him, and Casey got out of his car, with Wyatt doing the same. "What do you think?" Casey asked.

"I think we need to watch the place and see what's going on," Wyatt offered.

"But that's going to be hard out here. There aren't that many people, so a car sitting by the side of the road is going to be seen. Heck, it wouldn't surprise me if we had people coming up to us asking if we need help," Casey told Wyatt.

"Then we need to approach the house from the far side. The shrubs are overgrown, and we can simply check things out. It shouldn't be too hard to get close without being seen. We'll park around the corner and go through the woods."

Wyatt's idea seemed sound enough. Casey got back in his car and headed past the house again before turning the corner. Once he was sure he was out of sight, he parked and got out, then started through the small trees and around the underbrush, approaching the house from the east. Wyatt went farther north, and Casey caught glimpses of him through the trees.

A snap caught his attention, and he lowered his gaze to watch where he was going. About twenty feet later, a silvery gleam caught his eye. If the area hadn't been wet with dew, he probably would never have seen the line running along the ground. He paused, following the line toward a tree and then upward to a small bag of cans. Crude, but potentially effective.

Wyatt appeared in his line of sight, and he motioned for him to stop. Then Casey stepped back and headed for the cars once again. "What's going on?" Wyatt asked once he joined him.

"They have trip lines in there," Casey said. "I nearly set one off. It could be kids playing, but…."

"That tells us that something is going on," Wyatt said with a smile. "Okay, so you have the right house. What's the next step?"

"We check things out after dark and see what's going on. Out here it's dark as hell at night, so we should be able to get close to the house without too much trouble from the other side. While it's fairly open, there are a few trees and bushes we can use for cover." He also wanted to get a look inside some of the outbuildings to see what they might have stashed in them. But for now, they needed to leave the area before anyone got suspicious.

"Then I'll meet you here at nine and we'll see what's going on," Wyatt agreed, and they both got in their vehicles and left.

Casey was not known for his patience, so leaving was hard for him. He wanted to know what the hell was going on at that farm, and he sure as hell wanted to know if Jenn was there. Something felt off to him, but he couldn't quite figure out what it was. The trip lines were one thing, but there was something else about the place. He wished he dared drive by once more to take another look, but they had already gone by the house enough that if anyone was looking, they'd become suspicious.

He headed back toward town as a call came in, and he pulled his mind to where it needed to be.

"Do you have to go?" Jolie asked as they played Candyland on Bertie's living room floor with Beau.

"Yeah, I do." Casey picked a card and moved his piece to a pink square. "You two need to get ready for bed soon."

"Will you read us a story?" Beau asked, his big eyes pleading. The kids had been anxious all evening, and Casey wasn't sure why. Even Phillip didn't seem to be able to settle down.

"Finish up your game. It's almost bath time, and then you can all get ready for bed," Bertie said. Beau went ahead and picked a card and showed it to them, and Casey helped him move his piece.

"Did I win?" Beau asked as he reached the castle.

"Yes." Casey scooped him up. "You won, and Jolie almost won. I came in last. But that's okay. We had fun." He swung Beau around, and laughter filled the room. Then he handed Beau to Bertie and gave Jolie a turn. Casey was learning that there was no happier sound than childish laughter. It warmed the heart.

"Okay. You two can have a cookie before you go upstairs," Bertie said, and Phillip took the other two into the kitchen. "You be careful," Bertie told Casey, moving right in front of him. "I don't want anything to happen to you." The tension in the kids seemed to start with him.

"I'll be fine, I promise. This is what I do." And he needed to get to the bottom of this string of break-ins so folks could relax in their own homes. He was becoming more convinced after seeing Jenn and talking to the woman from the flea market that there was more going on than just thefts and selling stolen goods.

"When do you have to leave?" Bertie asked. "I still don't like this, but I understand you have to do what you need to." He kept looking outside. "I get that you do this all the time and that you know your job, but what I think is bothering me is that it's getting dark. You usually work during the day, and in my mind, you're safe then because it's light. I know that's probably stupid, but...." He moved into Casey's arms.

"About half an hour," Casey answered, hugging Bertie and keeping quiet. There was no need to explain that there was always danger, day or night. He didn't need to make Bertie worry more. "Why don't you get the kids ready for bed and I'll read them a story before I leave?" It was amazing how quickly he had been assimilated into this makeshift family and how quickly he had come to rely on it, even though he knew it was all an illusion. The kids weren't Bertie's, not permanently, and this family feeling was likely to dissolve once he got to the bottom of what was happening and Jenn got the help she needed.

The law was such that while they gave lip service to "the best interests of the children," basically it was written under the presumption that what was best for the kids was their mother. And in most cases, that was probably true. But in ones like this, they really should go against that presumption if they wanted to do the best for the kids. Casey held Bertie for a few more seconds, and then he went to look for the younger two in order to go upstairs, but Phillip stopped him.

"Are you going to put Mom in jail? You're doing a stakeout like on TV. Those usually end with people going to jail. Is that where Mom is going?"

Casey hadn't been prepared for that kind of question. It was insightful, but at the same time, a huge leap to conclusions. "I don't know. But if she does, we'll try to get her help." He sat down and patted the sofa cushion next to him. "I think that the men who robbed the garage of your house, and other people's garages and houses, might know where your mom is. So I'm trying to find them and hoping they'll lead me to her." He prayed that was enough to put Phillip at ease.

"But if she's done something wrong?" Phillip asked.

Casey wondered at the source of that question. Had Phillip seen his mother doing things she shouldn't? "I'm going to try to help your mom," Casey answered. "But if she has done things she shouldn't have, I'll listen to why she did them, and then I'll still try to help. I promise. But Phillip, if there's something you've seen or that you might know, you need to tell me."

Phillip sat there looking down at his shoes.

"Do you know where she is?"

He shook his head. "But she…. I saw her taking stuff that people brought to the house. I know she takes pills so she won't be crazy, but she took stuff other people brought." He lifted his gaze, eyes watery. "Is Mom on drugs?" His shoulders shook, and Casey hugged him. "Is she going to die?"

Oh God. "That's why I'm trying to find her. If she's on drugs, then Uncle Bertie and I will try to get her some help. But we have to find her first." Jesus, to think that a ten-year-old should have to deal with something like this. Casey couldn't imagine how terrible it must be to think your mother was on drugs. That must have scared Phillip half to death… and then to live with something like that day in and day out. The more he thought about it, the more chills raced up his spine. Somehow he had to bring this uncertainty to an end.

"Can you really do that?" Phillip asked. "The men who came, they were scary, and I stayed away."

"You did good, teaching the other kids to hide too." He rubbed Phillip's back to try to calm him. "I know what it's like to be scared sometimes. When I graduated high school, I tried college, but I wasn't smart like your uncle Bertie. My parents didn't understand about me being different, so I joined the Navy and got assigned to a big ship." He leaned close. "I hated it the entire time, and I let my fear rule how I felt. I was scared, so I didn't do other things very well."

"What did you do?"

"I learned to live with it. But you don't have to, because you have Uncle Bertie, and he's going to be there and make sure all of you are safe." Casey hugged him again.

"Will you be here to keep us safe too?" That worried smile was back.

"I'm going to do my best." He sure as heck hoped so. "Now, why don't you relax a little? It's probably about time for me to read the other two their story, and then I need to see what I can find out. Okay?" Phillip nodded, and Casey joined Bertie and the younger two for story time.

"SO, WHAT'S the plan?" Wyatt asked as they got out of the car.

Wyatt had driven them past the house, and the place was no longer quiet. At least six cars were in the drive and on the lawn. It seemed like a party of some sort, with a little music reaching outside the house, which was all closed up. The loudest sounds were coming from an old air-conditioning unit. They had cleared their recon with the lieutenant after showing him pictures of the outside. Their witness had even confirmed it as the house she had been to. They were under strict orders to get as close as they safely could, see what was going on, and then get out of there.

"Circle around to the side by the shed. We can only look, not enter. But with the position of those windows and that shed, I suspect we might be able to see inside from there."

"Do we split up?"

"No. Stay together, and watch for trip lines and stuff in the trees." He was anxious and excited. This was a chance for them to get to the bottom of what was going on. They had to get in and out, maybe take a few pictures, and then they could see about next steps.

"Okay. Then let's go. The house is right over there." They couldn't miss it, with every light on in the place.

Slowly, they made their way through the underbrush. Casey was thankful for long pants. At one point he saw something in the trees, and gently checked around until he found the trip line. They stepped over it and continued on. Casey hoped there weren't too many of those things, because getting lucky once was cool, but his luck wasn't going to hold for too many of those. Fortunately, Wyatt was eagle-eyed and spotted one as well. This time they shifted direction toward the back of the property. They reached the shed as light spilled out of the opening back door.

"I'll be right back," someone said as they stepped outside.

Casey pressed up against the side of the shed, holding still, not daring to move or even breathe as someone crossed the lawn and opened the door not five feet from where he stood. All they needed to do was peer around the side and he could be spotted. It was dark and he was in shadow, but still, he placed his hand on his gun, breathing as quietly as possible even though his heart pounded in his chest.

The man muttered something and rooted in the shed before closing the door and hefting something with him as he crossed back to the house. Casey began breathing again once the back door closed. He turned to Wyatt as the shed door slowly drifted open. It seemed whoever had come out hadn't latched it properly. Casey signaled for Wyatt to move around the back, and he used the door as a blind to sneak around the side. He peered inside a mostly full space.

He didn't dare shine a light, but in addition to some lawn equipment, he found piles of what looked like electronics. There was almost no light, and he strained his eyes to see more detail.

"Get out of there," Wyatt whispered, and Casey ducked out of the shed and around the corner.

"Stupid idiot. Can't even close a door," a man muttered just before Casey got around the corner. Then the door closed. More muttering followed and grew softer before the light from the back dimmed once more.

"I think we found some more of the stolen goods," Casey whispered. "I'm requesting a warrant to cover us." He sent messages back to the station, explaining what they had found and the need for a warrant.

"Then let's go. We were here checking out a tip and discovered a stash of electronics that we believed to be stolen goods in a shed with an open door. That's more than enough to allow us to look further."

Casey nodded but peered toward the house. "I can't see much in the windows. I want to see inside. Stay here. I'll be right back." He crouched low and stayed out of the shafts of light from the windows, easily making it to the back corner of the house. Then he crept low and stayed off to the side, peering at an angle from behind ratty curtains that hung past part of the window.

"Jesus," he breathed to himself. Within his line of sight, a large table dominated the room with only part of it visible, but what he saw nearly took his breath away: a packaging operation with people sitting around the table, heads down, with scales and small bags. That was more than enough to get whatever warrant he needed. Casey turned away and pressed against the side of the house as a woman came in from the next room. He chanced a glance as Jenn sat at the table with the others. She looked worse than when he'd seen her at the house. In fact, she seemed to be in the same clothes. Casey wondered if she had changed at all or if she was still wearing the same dirty stuff. Not that it mattered. She was working in a drug house.

Casey lowered himself to the ground and scurried away, once again staying out of the light. He reached the shed and motioned to Wyatt to head back toward his vehicle. They made it about halfway when a clatter rose to their right. One of them had tripped one of the lines, but they hurried farther away and out to the car.

Lights had come on outside the house, and people spilled out. Casey could hear them talking before someone told them to go inside and back to work. He and Wyatt stayed still by the car, ready to go at any sort of threat, but everything quieted, and Wyatt slipped behind the wheel. Casey pushed the car onto the road, and it started rolling down the slight incline. He hurried and got inside, the car rolling farther away, and then Wyatt started the engine and they slowly left the area.

"Do you want to call that in?" Wyatt asked.

Casey pulled out his phone and called their lieutenant. He explained what they saw and that they were out of there already.

"Did it look like they were packing up?" he asked. "I'd rather not send people in there at night."

"They seem to still be working right now." Casey paused and shared a look with Wyatt. "There were maybe six cars there tonight and only two this afternoon. So I think if we want to get as many people as possible, we need to go as soon as we can." He motioned for Wyatt to turn around. "We're going to drive by at speed to see what's going on. They had trip wires in the woods around the property, and we hit one. I want to make sure we didn't spook them. They were rudimentary, so I'm hoping they thought it was an animal or something. We stayed still and waited them out."

Wyatt stopped and did a three-point turn, then headed back the way they came. Casey watched ahead for cars pulling out but saw nothing. As they passed, the cars were all still in place, but the lights were on outside the house. Other than that, nothing had changed. Shit, he wished they had been more careful, but it was water under the bridge now.

"What does he want us to do?" Wyatt asked loudly.

"Stay in the area and find a place to watch the house until we get word that the warrant has been issued. I want to know if they are starting to pack up. I'm going to bring in a couple of teams, and they'll be out there within the hour."

The lieutenant ended the call, and Wyatt found a place around the corner where they could pull off the road and still see the house. Dousing all the lights, they sat low so if anyone passed, it would look like they had run off the road and the car was empty.

"I wish I had brought coffee and snacks," Wyatt muttered. "Food always makes something like this go faster."

"Yeah, but you rent coffee, and all we need is for someone to see us taking a leak as they pass. It's best to just sit and wait, I guess." Casey didn't want to sound like a dick or anything, so he actually tried to soften what he said. "I appreciate you doing this with me."

Wyatt turned to him, mouth open. "Who are you, and what the fuck have you done with Casey?" He grinned. "I know you don't mean to be a dick, but that's how you usually come across."

"I know. That's what Bertie told me too." They needed to do their job, and he wasn't sure this was the best time for a damned cop-to-cop talk.

"Then fix it," Wyatt told him. "I've seen you smile more this past week than I ever have, and you've been less assholeish than usual. I'm guessing that being happy is having an effect on you."

"I guess you could say that," Casey agreed and then smiled genuinely. "I'm happy, but I don't know if it's real. I mean, I know what I feel about Bertie, but there's so much going on. He's taking on three kids at almost a moment's notice, and…."

Wyatt shook his head. "No need to go on, for God's sake. If this is going to turn into some angst-ridden teen movie, you can stop. Bertie is a grown-up, and he knows what he feels, and if you're unsure, then ask him. I'm sure he'll tell you. And as for being happy, just enjoy it. The kids are a bigger issue. You need to make sure that you know what you want, because walking away would hurt them too."

"I know that."

"So just figure out what you want and stop worrying about the rest of it." He turned, and the seat crunched. "Look, if it was just you and Bertie, would you be happy?"

"Yes."

"Do you like the kids?"

"Yes. Of course I do. They're pretty amazing."

Wyatt shrugged. "Then what's the problem?"

Casey thought a minute before putting words to his fear. "What if they go back to their mother and Bertie decides he doesn't need me anymore? Everything could change at a moment's notice."

Wyatt shrugged again. "So it changes. You roll with it, because if you want to have someone special in your life who will be there through all the shit you need to wade through, then you accept that they'll change, you'll change, and I can guarantee the rest of the world will shift so fast you can barely hang on. And if someone is willing to stand by you through all that… then hold on for the ride of your life." Wyatt was either really poetic or just full of shit. Casey wasn't sure which.

"You know, you're a really big help," he responded with as much sarcasm as he could muster.

"You're welcome. Now can we go back to being cops, and you stop being an ass, and we'll get this damned job done?" He put his seat back like he was going to go to sleep or something. "What did you see when you looked inside that you didn't tell the lieutenant?"

"You mean the fact that Bertie's sister was in there packing that shit?" All he could think of was how hurt Bertie and those kids were going to be. How in the hell was he possibly going to make this one all right? "They've all been existing on some sort of hope, and now it's going to fall to me to rip that away. These kids aren't going to be seeing their mother anytime soon unless it's in an orange jumpsuit." He could just imagine trying to comfort Jolie, Beau, and Phillip once they found out.

"You know this isn't your fault," Wyatt said when Casey leaned forward. He picked up his phone. Two people hurried out of the house and started loading things in the cars.

"Lieutenant, there are people getting ready to leave. It looks like they're putting stuff in trunks," Casey reported just as sirens sounded. There was just enough light around the house for him to see people racing back into the house and then coming outside again.

"We got the warrant," Wyatt reported, reading their message. He started the engine and pulled forward, turned the corner, and parked right across the entrance to the drive, blocking in the cars. With culverts on either side of the drive, they were effectively shut in.

"You fucker! Get the hell out of the way," a man yelled as the sirens in stereo grew louder. He raced to one of the cars as additional troopers arrived and took up positions across the road and around them.

"Everyone come out of the house with your hands up," Sergeant Collins said, with Lieutenant Harper close by. "Now." Officers encircled the house, taking up places around the sides and back. "You are surrounded, and no one is going to escape. Come out slowly, hands up, and you won't be harmed."

Casey could feel the tension in the air. It crackled with it, and his leg muscles stiffened, ready to take action. He and Wyatt slipped out of the car and took positions behind it, watching the front door of the house. He half expected a shootout of some sort. He had no idea how many weapons were inside, but it was likely these people had been partaking of the products offered and weren't thinking clearly.

One shot rang out in the night, the recoil reverberating over the land and then dying away. Another followed, and then it was pandemonium. The front windows of the house shattered and crashed down, and shouts from outside battled with gunshots to be heard. The drug dealers on the back and side rushed forward; then yells and even a scream split the night.

Just as quickly as it started, the shooting was over and the night quieted once again. "The building is secured," came over a nearby radio, and Casey hurried inside.

The house was a wreck—windows gone, furniture overturned, blood spilling out on the floor from a dead man he didn't recognize. The dirty suspect lay on his side under the front window, a gun still clutched in his fingers. "Where are the rest of them?" Casey asked. "I'm Trooper Bombaro."

"Secured in the back. We cuffed everyone," a trooper whose name badge read Marcus answered. "You did good work getting us here fast." He scanned the room, and Casey did the same. An unopened brick of what appeared to be cocaine rested on the floor near the wall, and the table was on its side, spilling more onto the floor. Some kind of pills had also scattered everywhere when it fell.

"Thanks. Have they all been read their rights?" Casey asked.

"Being taken care of now," Marcus answered, and Casey waited until that was done before peering into the back room, where seven suspects sat on the floor against the walls. Jenn was second from the left, swaying slightly back and forth, her head falling forward. She looked unhurt as far as he could tell, but she might be in some kind of medical trouble. Casey backed out and turned to leave the house. There was absolutely nothing he could do for her, and the wheels of the law would turn on their own.

The man with the neck tattoo was a few people down. Casey checked for the guy he'd seen with the arm sleeve tattoos, but he wasn't among the group. He was disappointed they hadn't gotten him as well, but they'd find him one way or another. At least he hoped so.

"You did good," Sergeant Collins told him. "This is solid."

"I'm glad. But I'd pegged them as thieves."

"We believe our friend here was using the money from moving the stolen goods to set himself up in the narcotics business." He smiled. "Basically, we got lucky and shut the guy down permanently before he could really get started." He patted Casey on the shoulder. "You did a great job. There's additional goods in the basement that we're going to put into evidence, but I need you to try to match up the goods we have with the victims so we can eventually get their stuff back to them."

"I'll be on it first thing." It would be nice to have some good news for the theft victims. Though given the pace of the legal system, it could take months to get the things returned. He nearly turned away, but he paused. "I'm not sure how much product sampling has been going on, but I'm willing to bet that some of our suspects could be in some trouble."

Collins nodded. "We'll take care of it. You've had a long day. Go on home and get some rest. There's going to be plenty of work to get done tomorrow. Both of you," he added for Wyatt's benefit.

Casey returned to the car with Wyatt, and they headed back toward town. Casey sat in the passenger seat, taking a few minutes to send a note to Donald to let him know that Jenn had been found and that she was being taken into custody. He also sent a message to Bertie to tell him that he was going home and that he'd see him tomorrow when he was able.

"You know you should just go see him," Wyatt said as he pulled to a stop outside Casey's house.

"It's really late, and he needs to get up in the morning to get the kids ready to go." Casey got out. "Thanks for everything."

"Anytime."

Casey stepped back from the car, and Wyatt pulled away to head on home. Casey knew he was being a coward at the moment, but he needed some time to himself to figure out how he was going to break the news to Bertie about what had happened. And then what were they going to tell the kids? He had promised them that he'd do whatever he could to find their mother… and he had. Casey knew where she was and where she was going to be for the foreseeable future. That wasn't the issue.

I'm home and going to bed, he messaged Bertie, hoping he was sound asleep by now. He went into the kitchen, got something to drink, then went upstairs, cleaned up, set his phone on the charger, and climbed into bed.

He was exhausted but unable to sleep. Every time he tried, all he could see was the disappointment in Bertie's gaze, as well as three heartbroken kids, their huge eyes filled with tears as they asked him why he wasn't able to save their mommy.

CHAPTER 8

"THAT'S NOT how Casey does it," Beau said when Bertie handed him his plate with a piece of toast and a small amount of scrambled eggs.

"I'm sorry. Can you eat it anyway?" Bertie asked with as much patience as he could muster. He hadn't gotten much sleep last night. The bed had seemed so big and the room lonely and quiet without Casey's soft breathing nearby. He had quickly gotten used to that regular sound next to him, lulling him to sleep.

Beau looked at him as though he were crazy, and his lower lip quivered.

"Just eat, okay?" Phillip said. "Uncle Bertie is here to take care of us, and Casey is at his house because he has to go to work early. He'll be back. Just eat your brekky so we can all get going." He had already downed his food and was getting up from the table.

It seemed Phillip had met some boys his age at the Y and was excited for whatever was going to happen today. Bertie was pleased he seemed to be fitting in. Phillip was the one he worried about most.

Jolie ate steadily, while Beau picked at his eggs and finally took a bite, then another one, humphing the entire time as though the world was just too cruel. "Will Casey be here after school?" They had taken to calling it that for Beau because it sounded more grown-up.

"I don't know. He's working really hard right now, and we need to be as supportive as we can." Their messages last night had been quick, with Casey saying he was going home to bed. That had been a disappointment for Bertie. "But I'll talk to him today. Okay? You could draw pictures to show him how much you like him." Okay, so he was being a little shameless here, but he was worried about what he might have done or said to make Casey back away. Bertie knew he was being too sensitive and overly nervous. Things with Casey had been going well. Of course there was always the possibility that Casey had come to his senses and realized that things had been moving fast and that he really wasn't up for being part of Bertie's life. It was a lot to ask, a guy taking care of three kids. God, that was almost too much for him.

Bertie poured a cup of coffee and sat at the table, head drooping a little. Sleep was becoming a luxury, and it wasn't because the kids were up at night but because he kept waking and worrying that he was doing something wrong or that a noise in the house was one of the kids who might need him.

"Is this enough?" Beau asked as though he were being force-fed.

"Two more bites, okay?" Bertie asked, and Beau took a bite of eggs and one of toast. Then he got down from the table and ran away.

Bertie should probably have figured that eventually the newness of the situation was going to wear off and the kids were going to get testy and frustrated, even if they didn't have the words to express it.

Jolie ate her breakfast, and Bertie took care of the dishes. "Get ready to go," Bertie said. He checked Beau's pack to make sure everything was all set. Then came the hectic process of getting them all in the car and settled, beginning the morning run to day care and then the Y before going in to work to open the store and start the day there.

"THOSE ARE supposed to be the white daisies," Alice said gently.

Bertie blinked and set the white roses back in the bucket. He returned them to the cooler and got the daisies before finishing the arrangement and setting it in the cooler awaiting delivery.

"What's wrong with you today?" she whispered as she updated the screen to show the latest order she'd taken.

Bertie groaned and reached for his huge mug of coffee. "I'm okay."

"Welcome to parenthood. Too much coffee, not enough sleep."

"And if I eat one more chicken nugget, I'm going to grow feathers and lay eggs," he groused halfheartedly. The kids had been really good about eating the various things they'd had for dinner, but Bertie figured he needed to add something to the conversation. Maybe what he really needed was the chance to clear his head and get a decent night's sleep.

"You'll get used to it. All of it," she said gently. "It takes some time for everyone to get to know what to expect."

"And about that time, my sister is going to show up again to add a whole new level of chaos and upheaval to everyone's life. I know she isn't going to be able to take the kids even if she reappears today, but it's only going to mean court dates and more not knowing what's going to happen. The kids are already asking about their mom and when we're going to find her. Can you imagine how things are going to be when they do see her?" He clamped his eyes closed, willing his head not to ache at the mere notion.

"It sounds to me like you'd be a much better parent to them than she would," Alice said.

Bertie shrugged. He had no idea if he was really cut out to parent three kids. "I don't know. Yeah, I'd be better than Jenn, but would they be trading one kind of screw-up for another? What if I do something wrong?" The fear that lay mostly dormant because he was too busy decided to roar to life at that moment. He swallowed hard and tried not to let it overwhelm him.

"Parents don't get a manual. None of us does. After I had my first child, my mother came to stay with us for a month. She helped me through that tough period and nearly ended my marriage. Dennis was ready to take me and Gloria to Mexico to escape her. With the second, we were much more at ease, and by the third, it was old hat. We knew what we were doing. You didn't have that learning curve. But you stepped up and helped those kids. That's what counts. Just love them." She sighed. "That's all you really need to do. Punish when you have to, reward every chance you get, and most of all, listen." The phone rang, and she hurried back out front.

Bertie checked his phone for a message or a missed call before returning his attention to his work. He had to get these arrangements done and start the preparations for the weekend's weddings. He had already ordered the flowers he was going to need, as well as the supplies. He also had the time scheduled, along with drawings and layouts for each of them. Now it was a matter of planning and making sure that everything arrived on time. He got to work, his mind settling into the familiar creative rhythms.

For him, he was much less interested in doing the arrangements they made every day. He did them, of course, but weddings like the one coming up on Saturday were what he lived for. That was when he got to let his full creativity flow. This was a big one at the historic—as in George Washington worshipped there—Episcopal church on the square in town, and that meant he got to put on quite the floral show, especially with the budget the bride had authorized.

"Your phone keeps chiming," Millie said from the other work table. Bertie had set it on the corner of his and promptly ignored it.

He finished what he was doing and checked the message from Casey. *I need to see you as soon as possible.*

Do you want to come over after work? Is that soon enough? Bertie asked, as his stomach clenched and worry spiked through him. He had been dreading this type of message.

Yes. I'll see you then. I can't talk about this over text or phone, but I'll do my best to explain everything when I see you. This was bad. Bertie's mind went immediately to the worst, but he pulled it back. If Jenn was dead, then Casey most likely wouldn't have waited. No, this was either about the two of them, or God knows what. Bertie checked the time. He had hours before he was going to see Casey, and all he could do was trust that whatever was happening, Casey knew what he was doing.

Bertie did his best to keep his mind on his work and hoped the clock didn't slow to a tortoise pace. He could always dream.

"CASEY!" JOLIE called as soon as Bertie opened the door and Casey stepped inside, still in his uniform. She practically flew at him, and he caught her midleap, hugging her before setting her back down.

"Hey, sweetheart," he said gently, but his smile seemed forced, and he looked like he'd been dragged through a hedge backward. "Where are your brothers?"

"In the backyard, playing with Smidgen."

"She's been watching for you," Bertie explained as Jolie took Casey by the hand and dragged him into the kitchen, where she gave him her drawing and explained what everything was.

"I'll put this up in a place of honor," Casey told her.

"Why don't you go play with Phillip and Beau, and I'll be out there as soon as I can." Bertie barely had the door closed before he turned to Casey. "You're still on duty, aren't you?" There was something about the way he stood.

"Yeah, I am. I'll be off in about fifteen minutes. But I had to come here in an official capacity first." He pulled out a chair at a table covered with paper, crayons, and coloring books.

"So you aren't here to dump me or anything?" Bertie needed to know.

Casey put his hands on the table and reached for him, but stopped. "This is an official visit, and I'd never do something like that on work time." He held Bertie's gaze. "I don't intend to do that ever, if I can help it." He paused, relieved, and Bertie held his breath. "Look, last night after I left, I followed up on that farmhouse."

"You found it," Bertie said. "Was Jenn there?" A dose of excitement zinged through him.

"Yes, she was. Bertie, she's in pretty bad shape. She was at the farmhouse packaging pills into small sale-size packs. I'm not sure how much she's taken and over how much time, but we took her into custody last night. She had a bad reaction overnight, and now she's in the hospital in Harrisburg. They weren't equipped to treat her here in town. We administered the opiate overdose medication, Narcan, as soon as we found her having a bad reaction." Casey looked miserable.

Bertie swallowed hard. "You're telling me that Jenn...."

"Was working for a drug distributor and has overdosed. I'm afraid so. The last I heard she was stable, but I have limited information on her condition."

"I see." Bertie tried to wrap his mind around this. "What about the kids?"

"Well, I suspect that Child Services will move to remove all three of them from her care. And they may try to terminate her parental rights." Casey leaned forward. "There is no way she's going to be able to care for them in the short term. She will need to recover, and then she'll face charges for possession and intent to distribute, among others. There's little chance that she won't see jail time. How much, I don't know."

Bertie simply breathed slowly, in and out, trying to keep himself calm. "So I'm going to have the kids for a long time?" He tried not to let the fear creep into his voice, but he must have failed, because there was a startled noise from the doorway. He turned to see Phillip standing there, his eyes as black as a storm cloud.

"I...." He shook, and Bertie hurried over to him, but Phillip raced away through the house and out the front door.

"I'll go after him," Casey offered.

"You're still on duty," Bertie snapped. He wasn't necessarily angry at Casey, but he took his frustration out on him because he was an easy target. "Stay here." He hurried out the door and down the street.

Phillip had made it to the corner and seemed to be trying to figure out which way to go. Bertie hurried up to him.

"You don't want us either," he said, his face a mask of anger and hurt.

"Of course I want you," Bertie said. "Who wouldn't?" he asked, kneeling, hoping against hope that Phillip came to him. He hesitated and then went into his arms. Bertie hugged him tight as Phillip went to pieces right there.

"Mama didn't. She left us," Phillip said between tear-filled gasps. "And she's not coming back, is she? We're all foster kids now, like on TV." He held Bertie like he was all that stood between Phillip staying in one piece or flying all apart.

"Hey. Come back with me." He straightened and took Phillip's hand. "Let's go back to the house and we can tell you what's going on." God, this was the last thing he had wanted to do. Still, Phillip went with him, and Bertie counted it as a win.

"I'm going to change my clothes," Casey said once they returned, and Bertie nodded, leaving him to do what he needed to. Then Bertie sat Phillip on the sofa and took a place next to him, grateful the others were still outside playing.

"Do you know where Mama is?" Phillip asked.

"She's in the hospital right now, and they don't know if she's going to be okay or not. Your mom was taking too many things."

"Like drugs?" Phillip asked, and Bertie nodded. "Is she going to jail?"

"Probably. So that's why you and your brother and sister are going to be staying here."

"But you don't want us," Phillip said, sticking out his lower lip.

"Of course I do. There was never a minute that I didn't want all three of you. I know your mom is going to be having a very hard time of it, but that doesn't mean that I don't want you and that we aren't going to be a family." He hugged him again just as a strong hand rested on his shoulder. Bertie reveled in both sensations, hoping that he could have the family that the hug represented, and the support, care, and maybe love, that the touch of strength held. He wanted it all but wasn't sure if it was possible. Things didn't seem to be working out lately.

"But when she comes back?" Phillip asked.

"I don't know what will happen when she gets better. That isn't for us to say. What I hope is that she'll be better and able to take care of all of you. But if she isn't, then you'll have a home here with me. Always. Is that okay?" Bertie asked, and Phillip went into his arms again, holding him hard.

He lifted his gaze as Casey looked back at him, smiling slightly. God, he hoped he was up to a task like this. "Can I go back outside?" Phillip asked. Bertie nodded, and Phillip wiped his eyes before going back out to where the others were playing.

"What am I going to do?" Bertie asked.

"That all depends on what you want," Casey said, and then it was his turn to be hugged.

"I can't let those kids go. I can't."

"Then what has you so scared?" Casey asked. "I know you, and I know you would never hurt those kids. So the only thing left is fear."

Bertie sniffed. "It's going to sound awful. But what if Jenn does get better? Then the kids will return to her and I'll be alone again." He buried his face against Casey's neck. "I love all of them, but it could just get ripped away at some point." Casey held him tighter just as Bertie was afraid he was going to go to pieces. "What am I going to do?"

"Hey. We're going to call Donald and see what he says. But for right now, Jenn is in no position to care for anyone, not even herself. Which means the kids are going to be with you for the foreseeable future. What Jenn has done isn't something any court is going to overlook. She left her children so she could pursue a need for drugs and the money to get the drugs. Who knows what she's done in order to feed the need?" He sighed. "But no judge is going to return those kids to her. And she's going to have to demonstrate to a lot of people that she's able to care for them."

Bertie nodded. "But…."

"All you can do is take it one day at a time and give all of them your love and care." He stepped back slightly, cupping Bertie's cheeks in his warm hands. "If anyone is capable of loving and caring for these kids, it's you. They adore their uncle." He leaned closer. "And so do I."

Bertie smiled gently. "I guess I'd better call Donald and find out what the next steps are. Right now they're here under some emergency order, but it looks like they'll need to be with me for a while. I wonder if I need to be registered as a foster parent or something."

"I don't know. But you're their closest family, so it may not be necessary because of that. I don't really know. But Donald does, and I know he'll help you." Casey pulled out his phone and made a call, then handed it to Bertie. "It's Donald."

Bertie didn't know whether to be grateful or mad. He settled on grateful, because Casey was trying to help. "Hey," he said, a little out of breath from the emotional whiplash. "Umm, apparently my sister is currently in the hospital, and if she recovers, she'll be in police custody. The kids are going to need care long-term."

"Are you prepared to do that?"

"Yes," he answered immediately. "But I don't know what the rules are or what I'm going to have to do."

"I'll get a visit from a social worker set up. They can help you. Are any of the kids sharing a room?"

"The two younger ones are in the same bed because it's all I have," Bertie answered.

"Okay. Then I'd suggest bunk beds. They can share a room, but they should each have their own bed. That's a pretty big deal. I'll contact you tomorrow to set up an appointment. Marie is wonderful. She's good with kids, and she understands situations like yours." Bertie sighed. "Is there anything else you need? Are they doing well in day care?"

"Phillip loves the Y program you helped us with. But I'm going to have to get the kids enrolled for school in the fall. What do I need for that?"

"I'll have Marie bring all that information as well. They'll be in the same district, but different schools. We can also arrange for Beau to start a preschool program." He paused, and it sounded like he was typing. "I'm sending her a note right now."

"Thank you. I just need to know what's going to happen, and so do the kids." He sighed, and Casey took his hand. "What do I tell them? Phillip is old enough to understand part of it, but the other two just ask for their mother." That was the nearly impossible part. "How do I help them understand?"

Donald was quiet for a moment. "My suggestion is that you tell them as much of the truth as you think they can handle. Right now, you could tell them that their mother is sick and that she is going to need some help. Then tell them that you're going to look after them and love them." Damn, Donald's voice sounded as though it was breaking. Bertie held the phone, on the verge of tears himself. "Just be there for them and follow your instincts. If you have questions, I'm here, and so is Maria. We'll do whatever we can."

Bertie found himself nodding as they ended the call. He fell into Casey's arms, burying his face in his neck, letting out the fear and hurt that had built up. Mostly he cried for the kids and the fact that they weren't going to have a mother to take care of them, and the pain that was sure to come.

"ARE THEY all in bed?" Bertie asked once Casey came back downstairs, Smidgen following him.

"Phillip is reading, and the other two are sound asleep, but it took three stories this time." Casey sat next to him on the sofa, and the dog jumped up and settled on his lap.

Bertie absently stroked his ears, letting the contentment he always felt with his dog settle deep inside. "Then I'll go up and talk to Phillip before he goes to sleep." His back ached, and he knew it was all from stress, but he got up, with the dog following, and quietly knocked on Phillip's door. "Hey, are you doing okay?"

"I guess," he answered.

Bertie sat on the side of his bed. Smidgen jumped onto the bed, nudging Phillip's hand for attention.

"What's going to happen to Mom?" One thing was for sure, Smidgen always seemed to know when someone needed him. It was Bertie's dog's superpower, and these kids were in need of all the comfort any of them could provide.

"I don't know. The doctors say that she seemed to be improving, and that's good." The latest update was that she was improving physically, but they were unsure of her mental state or what the overdose had done to her mind. "We'll take things as they come."

"Can we visit?" He bit his lower lip.

"I hope so, eventually. Right now she's sleeping all the time, but as she gets better, you'll all be able to go up and see her." God knows how that visit was going to end up, and Bertie would like to put it off for as long as possible. But the kids needed to see their mom to know she was alive. Bertie had no idea if Jenn was ever going to be okay again. "Why don't you turn out the light and go to sleep?" he said softly and tucked Phillip in.

"Good night, buddy," Casey said from the doorway.

Phillip rolled over to face them. "Is my mom going to go to jail?" Sometimes the kid was way too smart for his own good. "I know she was doing bad things."

"I don't know," Bertie said.

Phillip shifted his gaze to Casey, who said, "It's too soon to tell. A lot depends on when she gets well." Bertie hugged Phillip, and Smidgen got comfortable.

"We promise to tell you the truth when we know what's going to happen," Bertie told him. "Now go ahead and get some sleep."

Phillip settled in bed. Bertie lightly stroked the dog and then got up, and he and Casey quietly left the room. Bertie checked on the other two before going downstairs.

"Is it bad that I want them?" Bertie asked. "I know they're Jenn's kids, but does it make me a bad person that I sort of hope that she isn't able to care for them? I don't want anything to happen to Jenn, but these kids deserve so much more than a future dictated by her. They need to be happy and have time to play, not worry about their mother's moods and what she's going to do next."

"Hey, it doesn't make you bad for wanting the best for them. And we all have to admit that your sister has made some very bad decisions in her life. And those decisions affect more than just her, whether she sees that or not."

"So you're saying…."

Casey took his hand, entwining their fingers. "No. That doesn't make you a bad person. I promise." He shifted a little closer. "You know, the house is quiet, the kids are in bed, and it's just the two of us."

Bertie grinned. "What do you want to talk about? Work? You could tell me about your day." He leaned closer as Casey groaned. "Not that. Then I could tell you about my day. I know, we could talk about growing orchids. You have some beautiful flowers, and I love flowers. Maybe you and I could have a very deep conversation."

Casey nodded. "I see. You want to talk dirty." Now it was Bertie's turn to groan. "You know, I use my own special mix for my plants."

Bertie shook his head. "I wanted to talk *dirty*… not dirt. But whatever turns you on. I'm just as kinky as the next guy, and if mud is what does it for you, then maybe I can try to help. Though the chafing might be a little too much."

"You're funny, and I'll have you know I was never that kinky. Not even back in high school when a light breeze would give me a stiffy." He bumped Bertie's shoulder. He paused and dug around in his shirt, then pulled out a card. "This is the number of the nurses' station at the hospital where Jenn is. I told them that you were her brother and that you had permission to get basic updates on her condition."

"But can they tell me anything? With all the privacy laws and stuff, it's hard to get information," Bertie said.

"Yes. But she's in police custody, and they aren't going to tell you anything more than if she's awake or not. I also arranged with them so that if she's awake, you can speak with her. Anything said will be recorded, so there won't be any privacy, but it will be a chance for you to reassure her that the kids are okay." Casey seemed drawn and tired.

"Okay... that's enough about Jenn and the kids." Bertie's shoulders ached from the burden placed on them. "Tell me something about yourself that I don't know. You said you hated the Navy, but there must have been something you liked." Bertie smirked. "Did you meet someone? Have a great seafood diet?" He snickered at the old-time gay slang for sailors.

Casey paused. "You know, there were times. I was on one of the big ships, a carrier, and we were at sea for months on end. I worked in the bowels of the ship in communications, so my quarters and work were just a few steps away from each other. Basically I watched screens for my shifts. Day or night, it was all the same. But there were times when I got to walk the deck, especially at night. I got to look up at all the stars, which seemed to go on forever. Where we were, even the stars were unfamiliar, depending on our location, but in the middle of the ocean with nothing else around, the stars went all the way to the water, and there were instances when it was hard to tell where the sky ended and the water began." He sat back and seemed to relax.

"I thought you didn't like it."

"Oh, I didn't. Because most of the days I never saw the sun. If there were any sort of flight operations in progress, which was a lot of the time, I was relegated to my little part of the ship because I had to be near my cubicle of a room. Can you imagine not even knowing if it was day or night other than by the clock on the wall because you went weeks without seeing the sun? There were times when I nearly went out of my mind. I used to go up to a few spots to stand in the sun or look at the moon. Then I'd go back down to my little hole."

"That sounds kind of harsh."

"It's hard for most people to understand. My personal space was the base of my bed and only that. So there were regulations on exactly how to pack it so everything would fit perfectly. As for something that wasn't regulation, there was no room. Not that there was anywhere to buy anything unless we were putting in at a base. Then we could go ashore, but anything we bought had to be eaten, drunk, or shipped home. But there wasn't really much of a place to do that, so I ate and drank my way through any port stop, got back on the ship, and went back to my windowless room."

Bertie could understand why Casey had left as soon as he could. "What about people you met?"

"A ship like that is kind of like a sexual tension pressure cooker. There are all kinds of rules about who you can and can't get to know… if you understand what I mean. Mostly the rule is just say no, because getting to know someone is a recipe for disaster. You meet someone and get to know them, and a month later they get transferred or you get moved to a different ship and never see them again. I had friendships, but most of those lasted until one of us was transferred. We'd see each other later and we'd have a drink or dinner and then go our separate ways." Casey shrugged.

"You don't have any friends from your time at sea?" That seemed kind of sad. An entire chapter of someone's life wiped away as though it didn't exist. Like it hadn't left a mark on Casey's life, when it definitely had.

"I do. But life goes on." He smiled. "What about you? What's something I don't know? Something that you don't tell everyone." He leaned closer. "What's Bertie's secret?"

Bertie chuckled as he held Casey's gaze. "If I tell you, I might be confessing to a crime." He put his hands in front of him. "Will you be slapping the cuffs on me?" he asked, only partly teasing.

"What did you do? Share a joint with someone?" Casey retorted, chuckling slightly.

"No. I was a bit of a wild kid. I was different, especially in high school. Look at me. It's not like anyone didn't know I was gay—they all did. I got hassled for it, and after a while, I got tired of it. I was a teenager with raging hormones, hurt, and I didn't see any way out of it." He sat back, and Casey put an arm around him.

"What did you do?" Bertie could almost tell what Casey was thinking.

"Not that. I didn't hurt myself or anything. Instead, I got angry and decided to get even." The tension and pain from that time seemed to roar back to life, and Bertie went rigid with it. "I found out where my bullies lived, and when they were away at one of their games, I went around and bashed their mailboxes. Once I found my dad's air pistol and used it to shoot out a few of their windows. More than once I waited outside the school while they were at practice or at an activity and used an ice pick to puncture the side of their tires. I was really out of control. Every time someone would hurt me, I'd strike back as hard as I could."

Casey stared at him. "God...."

"I know. I was just a ball of rage and hurt. The thing was that it didn't get me anywhere. They still bullied me and were pissed because their shit was getting broken." He shook his head. "My parents didn't know what to do, and I didn't either. I got more and more unhappy." He took a deep breath, held it, and then sighed. "My grandmother stepped in. She was well into her eighties, but she saw what was happening."

"What did she do?" Casey asked quietly, tightening his hold a little.

Bertie closed his eyes. "She went down to the school, leaning on her cane, and read the principal the riot act. Apparently she had been his babysitter years before, and I don't know what the hell she said, but the next time I was bullied, one of the teachers saw it and there was hell to pay for the bullies. One lost his spot on the basketball team, and others were suspended. The hammer came down hard, and it changed the atmosphere in the school... sort of. The kids being bullied could relax, and the teachers were all on the lookout for that behavior. As for me, I was able to let go of some of the anger. Kids still picked on me sometimes, but I found some strength inside myself. My grandmother had stood up for me, and that meant I had someone in my corner." He turned to Casey. "I never realized how important that was until then. My mom and dad didn't know what to do, but Grandma sure did." Bertie lowered his gaze. "She died a few months after that."

"Did she know about you?" Casey asked. "Did you ever tell her?" He seemed to gentle, and Bertie leaned closer, taking the comfort he offered.

"That was a very rough time in my life, and things could have turned out so very differently if she hadn't stepped in. I know that." He smiled slightly. "Yeah, Grandma knew. I don't think my parents did. They just thought I was going through a phase or something. But she knew and told me that I had to be who I was. That was difficult, because Mom and Dad were going to have such a hard time with it. She knew it, and so did I. But she gave me the courage to eventually tell them... and bring about a whole new level of discomfort and things we didn't talk about." He humphed softly. "I was still trying to figure things out when

I met you for the first time, and I didn't know what to do about it. By the time I got up the courage, you were gone and off in the Navy."

"Did you really miss me?" Casey asked, drawing closer.

"Are you kidding? That second semester, I looked for you in the cafeteria and in classes, but you were gone. I had figured things out and wanted to talk to you. I'd made up my mind that I was going to be myself and be out… let the chips fall where they may. I had even planned to ask you out on a date. But you were gone, and I had no idea where you were."

"I'm sorry, for so many reasons. School was such a struggle for me. I kept trying to find where I fit in, and that wasn't it. I figured I'd go into the service, and since my granddad was in the Navy and always talked about how great it was, I followed in his footsteps. As much as I didn't like it, I learned a lot about myself. I wasn't going to find where I fit in by making stupid, rash decisions. So I sat down and thought about the things I liked and what I wanted to do. I grew up a lot in the Navy, and I thought law enforcement might fit. I went and talked to officers and people at the academy. Only then did I sign up, and that's when I found part of myself." He paused. "The rest of it I located when I went to return a lost purse and found three kids… and later their uncle. I wasn't expecting anything like that. And there you were."

A snap from outside had Casey pushing Bertie to the floor. "Stay down," he ordered, and Bertie lay flat in front of the sofa while Casey crawled toward the window. Bertie peered around the edge of the sofa as Casey glanced outside for the briefest moment. The snap happened again, and Casey returned.

"What's going on?" Bertie asked.

"Sorry. Some kids are out front, and one of them banged one of the light poles. The noise sounded like a shot, and…." He returned, and Bertie got back up.

"Does that happen often?" Bertie asked, brushing off his shirt. Man, he really needed to do some cleaning. He hadn't had time lately, and the place needed a little attention.

"No. But a gunshot has a certain sound, a feeling to it, and when it happens, I react. I didn't mean to scare you." He sat back on the sofa. "Where were we?" he asked.

Bertie shrugged. "I don't know. After ending up on the floor, and not in a really good way, if you know what I mean…." He couldn't help smirking. "My heart is still racing, and I doubt I can sleep after that."

Casey pulled him close. "Sleep—at least right away—wasn't what I had in mind."

"I get that. And I appreciate you talking and keeping my mind off it, but I can't help worrying about Jenn and what's going to happen to her." He watched Casey's gaze, which had suddenly receded like a wall had gone up, the warmth in his eyes fading. "You need to tell me what's happening."

"It's a little complicated. But basically we have enough to put the people behind this drug ring your sister got herself involved with out of commission. We have the people involved. But some of the people behind it got away. We're trying to track them down, but no one is talking. The people who might know have lawyered up and are refusing to talk to us. Which is their right."

"And you're hoping Jenn might know something," Bertie supplied.

"Yeah. But she's still in a hospital bed and is in no shape to talk to anyone." He closed his eyes. "There are things I'm not at liberty to talk about. This is an active investigation, and it involves your sister. So I have to put some distance between you and it for your sake and for mine, as well as Jenn's. She could hold the key to who is behind this. The man the kids saw at their house, as well as the one I saw at the market, with the sleeve tattoos, hasn't been found yet. His partner will say nothing, and that's part of what leads me to believe he must be the one with the power and connections. The others are all afraid of him, and whenever he's mentioned, they clamp their lips closed. We have a name, Tito, and that's all. It's a nickname, and we can get nothing else, no matter how we lean on them."

"You know Jenn can be stubborn as hell," Bertie told him.

"Yes. But she's also a mother, and helping us could mean seeing her kids again," Casey said.

Bertie pulled away. "You'd do that? Use the kids that way? If she helped, you would agree to give her the kids back after all she's done?" Bertie was aghast. He jumped to his feet and paced the room. "Are you that—?" He didn't have the words to express how he felt.

"That isn't how the law works," Casey told him. "We don't have that kind of power, nor do we get to make those decisions. But cooperation would look good for her if and when she tried to become part of her children's lives again." He sounded so reasonable, and Bertie wasn't in the mood for reason. He was tired, cranky, and if he was honest, feeling a little put-upon. He loved the kids, but suddenly he was expected to step in and act like a parent when he didn't have any experience with this. Hell, up until a short time ago, he had never given having kids a thought, and now he had three of them living in his house. Maybe he was being selfish, but it was a lot to ask of someone. Now Casey was talking about using them as leverage.

"Then what are you saying?" He leaned close. "Because from where I'm standing, it sounds a lot like using Jolie, Beau, and Phillip as bargaining chips with Jenn. I know you want her to talk to you, but I won't have the kids put at risk for any reason, and that means that whatever deals you make with her had better not involve them, no matter what anyone down at that station might think."

"Or what?" Casey asked, an amused smirk on his lips.

"Heads will roll. I'll take it to the news media. They'll eat that shit up, and let me tell you, the police will wish they were never born by the time I'm finished with them. Those kids have been through so much, and I won't have them used in any way." He had one hell of a head of steam going, and Casey wasn't sure what was going on with him.

"I promise that no one is going to do anything that will hurt them," Casey said, putting one hand up like he was a Boy Scout.

Bertie glared. "They had better not." He put both hands on his hips. "What?" he asked when Casey just sat there.

"And you were worried about being a good parent," Casey said. "You went a little off the deep end there. You know I care for those kids and would never hurt them." The sadness in his voice cut through Bertie's thoughts. "I think you know me better than that."

"Do I really?" Bertie asked. "I know you like the kids, and I doubt you'd ever do anything on purpose to hurt any of us, but you and I knew each other in college, and then we met again a little while ago." He paused because he wasn't making himself clear, and he felt like he was on verbal quicksand. "I know that you'd never hurt the kids, but you have to understand that you and I don't have a long history. It sounded like you were going to try to trade the kids for Jenn's cooperation, and I—"

"You turned into a tiger," Casey interrupted. "You thought I was going to hurt the kids and went full parental tiger on me." He looked almost amused.

"Why aren't you upset?" Bertie wondered if Casey was making fun of him.

"Because you turned into a parent, and no one should fault you for that. Standing up for the kids is something worthy and amazing. You don't need to worry on my behalf or about the department. But if we can get Jenn to tell us what we need to know, then everyone in town, including the kids, will be safer with this man off the streets. It's that simple."

Bertie went cold. "Do you think they're in danger? Is this guy going to come after them for some reason?" Okay, he needed to step back and get his head out of the plot of one of those cop shows. He was letting his worry overwhelm his logic and reason. The kids were with him, and they were safe.

"There is no reason to believe that he knows about the kids or has any interest in them." Casey pulled him close. "Just relax, because no one is going to hurt you or them while I'm around."

Bertie closed his eyes, and his mind finally stopped its constant spinning in circles. "How can you be so sure? Do you think this guy is going to be afraid of you because you're a cop?"

"Are you kidding? I think he's going to be scared because I'm big and strong. But the one he should be afraid of is you, tiger." Casey made this growly noise in his throat and then kissed him. The pressure on his lips hardened, and Bertie let Casey carry him along. He had spent so much time worrying about what was going to happen to the kids, to Jenn, even to himself and their future. It was nice to have someone want to take care of him.

"You're so damned funny," Bertie retorted once Casey pulled back.

"Maybe." He reached over to turn out the lights.

"What are you doing that for?" Bertie asked.

Casey rolled his eyes and took Bertie's hand. "Come on. I think it's time for a little you and me alone." He turned out the next lights and headed for the stairs. "We've played games and colored pictures, fed the kids, and gotten them into bed. Now I think it's time that I tucked you in for the night."

CHAPTER 9

BERTIE CHUCKLED as Casey closed the bedroom door. "I don't think I've had anyone tuck me into bed since I was eight years old."

Casey pressed him back onto the bed. "Okay, then I could fuck you into bed. Does that sound better?" He sure as hell hoped so, because that sounded like an amazing plan to him. Casey was already removing his shirt as Bertie's eyes darkened, and damned if Bertie didn't lick his pink lips.

Bertie's breath hitched. "Damn... umm... yes."

Casey continued undressing, and Bertie held still, watching... no, staring. "Is something wrong? Did I get food on me?"

"No." Bertie didn't turn away. "I just like watching you." He swallowed hard. "If I close my eyes, I can see you in college. You had this permanent bedhead that I thought was so adorable, and those clothes that just hinted at what you had under them. I used to spend as much time undressing you in my mind as I did studying. I'll have you know...." Bertie glided closer. "My grades went up a full point that second semester because you weren't there to fuel my imagination."

"Do you wish we were still back in college?" Casey asked as he kicked off his shoes.

"Not for a minute. That person was young, finding his way, and wild. This one is hot, sexy, and confident, which goes right along with the other two. He's also strong and steady in all the ways that count."

Casey scowled. "But I want to be wild." He slipped off his pants and prowled onto the bed, kissing Bertie back down into the mattress. "I want to be really out-of-this-world wild, like I was in college. If I had thought I had a chance back then, I'd have gone all caveman on you."

"Well, now's your chance. You can be as wild and energetic as you want... as long as you're quiet."

"So no crazy Tarzan yells?" he asked with his best mock pout. "And I can't make you scream either?" He humphed softly.

Bertie wound his arms around Casey's neck. "Nope. No screaming." He kissed him, tugging Casey downward. "But you can make me *want* to scream and bite the pillow. You can even make me go out of my mind and bite my own fist to keep from waking half the neighborhood." He held Casey tighter. "That you can most definitely do."

Casey shivered, and it wasn't from the air-conditioning. Then he tugged Bertie's shirt up and off and ran his fingers over his heated skin. There was something about this slight but sexy man that got his motor running like no one else. After years apart, Casey still wondered how he could ever have turned his back. Yet as Bertie had said, what came before was what allowed them to find each other again. And Casey had no intention of letting Bertie go this time. "Then how about we see what kind of self-control you really have."

It took all of his not to attack Bertie as he took care of the last of their clothes. Then all bets were off, because damn, Bertie tasted good and felt even better. "Casey...."

He hummed as he sucked at the base of Bertie's neck, making him writhe on the bedding. "Uh-huh." He didn't want to stop for a second. He slid down Bertie's body and took his cock between his lips. Bertie groaned, and whatever he wanted to say seemed lost in the clouds of desire that filled the room.

Bertie was like a wild man, a tiger. Casey thought he'd be able to take control, but he should have thought again. Bertie was like a live wire, all energy and motion. Bertie raised his hips, thrusting upward, taking Casey along for the ride, which he was more than happy to go along with. When he pulled back to catch his breath, Bertie took advantage, pouncing and pressing him back on the mattress.

"Did you think I was going to let you run things?" Bertie asked, his eyes a little wild.

That was exactly what he thought.

"Did you ever hear of topping from the bottom? Well, honey, meet your toppy bottom." Bertie kissed him hard, tweaking a nipple nearly to the point of pain and then backing off just enough to add the zing to Casey's already rising excitement. Holy hell, he was already flying, and all Bertie had done was kiss him. Swallowing a groan, he met Bertie's fiery gaze, taking a second to wonder when the gentle man he'd been with these past few weeks had been taken over by the tiger straddling him.

"Sweetheart, you can be whatever you want," Casey told him, holding Bertie tightly, before kissing him with as much energy as Bertie was putting out.

In seconds the room became electric, the very air infused with enough energy to raise the hair on his arms. He quaked on the bed, holding still and closing his eyes as Bertie slid downward, his hot lips and tongue blazing a trail over his chest and down his belly that he could still feel after Bertie had passed. No one had ever made him feel this alive, happy, and complete. Casey had always thought that those kinds of feelings were only found in books—fairy tales just as fictional as the stories they were in. But now he knew they were real and that they could happen to someone as ordinary as he was. It really was possible for someone to be your other half.

"Bertie... love...," he whispered as his cock throbbed with anticipatory excitement. He held his breath, clamping his eyes closed, willing Bertie to just take him. Instead, Bertie seemed intent on teasing him, sucking at the base of his hip and along his outer thigh. Casey wasn't sure how much more he could take. He rocked his hips slightly to try to encourage Bertie to give him what he wanted. "Please...."

"What is it you want?" Bertie asked with a touch of humor in his voice. "Don't use your words. Tell me with your body."

Casey widened his eyes and tried to think how he could do that. His body was already on edge, and all he could think of to do was thrust his hips upward and hold them there. Bertie got the message, smiling and taking him deep in one swift motion that stole Casey's breath. Damn, Bertie knew exactly what he was doing. The wet heat surrounding him was almost more than he could take. Bertie bobbed his head, sucking hard, sending Casey into orbit.

"Sweetheart," Casey gasped, "what are you trying to do to me?" He didn't get an answer to his question. Not that he expected one. But danged if Bertie didn't take him deep and hold still, sending a zing of excitement racing through him to the point he nearly lost it.

Casey held his hand over his mouth, the urge to cry out almost overwhelming. All he wanted was a way to release the passion that built from within. But he didn't dare. The last thing he wanted was for Bertie to stop, and the fastest way for that to happen was to wake the kids. He had to be quiet, and if that meant his eyes popped out of his head, so be it. "You're killing me here."

Bertie pulled away, Casey's cock bouncing on his belly as Bertie lay on top of him, kissing Casey furiously. It was a stunning bit of self-control on both their parts. "Do you think you can lie there and be still?"

"What for?" Casey asked as Bertie reached to the bedside table.

Bertie waved a condom in front of his eyes. "You only get to do this if you lie still. I want to be the one in charge."

Casey nodded. By this point, if Bertie told him he wanted Casey to sign over his house and car, he'd damned well do it. Bertie unwrapped the condom and rolled it down Casey's length. Casey hissed at the amazing sensation before Bertie got into position, used some lube, and then sank down on him.

The pressure around him was sublime. Casey did his best to hold still even though every cell in his body urged him forward. He wanted Bertie so badly. The two of them together were magical, and Casey wanted as much of Bertie as he was willing to give. As Bertie sank deeper, he rested his hands on Casey's chest. "Are you trying to blow my head clean off?" Casey managed to whisper while clutching the bedding.

"No." Bertie stilled his motions, staring into his eyes. For a few seconds Casey could almost see the answers to all of life's question in Bertie's eyes, and he wished he could get a hold on them before they flashed away as quickly as they'd come. Still, he had never had a connection like that with anyone.

"Well, you're doing a damned fine impression," Casey whispered, his throat a little dry, and he couldn't seem to swallow enough to keep it wet. That was what Bertie did to him—took away his body's ability do normal things, because he was so centered on Bertie and the way he made him feel.

"Then how about this?" Bertie leaned close, rolling his hips slightly, and damned if Casey's eyes didn't roll into the back of his head.

"Fuck," Casey whispered breathily, barely able to form words. Not that talking was the first thing on his mind.

"Remember, you promised to stay still." Bertie rolled his hips again, and Casey was reminded of a rodeo he'd seen on TV once and how the cowboys used their hips. Except they had nothing on how beautiful and graceful Bertie was. Casey watched him as he leaned back slightly, all sleek muscle and golden skin, eyes as big and deep as the sky just before the sun faded away. He ran his hands along Bertie's thighs, the muscles bunching and releasing under his palms. Damn, that was a sight he would never get tired of for as long as he lived, and when Bertie clenched around him, Casey thought he was already on his way to heaven, or as close to it as he could get on earth.

Casey honestly had no idea how much longer he was going to be able to control himself. The way Bertie rode him and the way he seemed to glow as the low light glistened off his sweat-dampened skin—all of it combined into this perfect erotic mixture. Add in the deep muskiness of his scent and Casey was already flying.

"Damn, you have to be the most stunning thing I have ever seen in my life," Casey said between gritted teeth. "Right here, right now, with you… I…." Casey growled and grew silent.

Bertie leaned forward, cupping Casey's cheeks. "I know what you mean to say, and you aren't the only one." Bertie kissed him hard. "You aren't the only one who seems to have found something here. I thought you were gone forever, and then at one of the most difficult times of my life, you show up again."

Casey smiled. "Like a knight in shining armor."

Bertie didn't answer. Instead, he rolled his hips once more, only this time, he found the most amazing rhythm that drove Casey absolutely out of his mind.

He was determined to wait and hold out as long as he could. Casey grew enthralled as Bertie slowly stroked himself, and as Bertie's movements grew more ragged, Casey used every ounce of self-control he had left to hold off. The sight and sensation of Bertie's climax brought on Casey's in a wave of passion too big for him to ever be able to contain, and Casey rode it for all he was worth until he lay spent and unable to move, holding Bertie in his arms. Casey never wanted to move again. If he could stay right here, like this, forever, he'd be a happy man.

"Hey, hot stuff," Bertie whispered into the dark room. "You know we need to get up or we'll be stuck together permanently."

"You talk like that's a bad thing." He tightened his hold, and Bertie settled against him.

"Definitely not. But you see, we'd have to explain being stuck to the kids, and getting dressed would be a problem. Now, there are many things I hope to teach those kids, but what our bare asses look like is most definitely not one of them. Beau sometimes searches the house for his mom and then comes to my room, half asleep, crying because he can't find her."

"Damn," Casey breathed. "The bad part is that they aren't going to be able to find her at home for quite some time." He slipped out of the bed and went to the bathroom, cleaned himself up, and came back with a cloth for Bertie to do the same. Once he returned the cloth to the bathroom, he pulled on some underwear and went back downstairs. Smidgen came out of Phillip's room and followed him downstairs, padding around as he checked the doors and windows before looking at his phone one last time.

He found a message from Wyatt to call him. "Hey. Is it too late?" he asked as soon as the call connected.

"No. I'm glad you didn't wait. We've got a problem. One of our suspects, Brian Hodges, already posted bail and is back out on the street. The guy with the bobcat tattoo. We know his mother arranged for him to get out, and I suspect he and his friend Wilkinson are going to try to intimidate anyone who might be able to testify against them. All of our suspects are scared shitless."

"Yeah, I know."

Wyatt cleared his throat. "One thing we were able to piece together is that Jenn was involved with Hodges in some way, and he's aware that she has kids. Jenn is still unconscious, and we have guards on her around the clock. If she regains consciousness, we might be able to get her to talk."

Casey felt himself pale. "And if they know about the kids, then they could possibly get it in their little pea brains that the one way to get to Jenn is to make sure she knows they can get to the kids."

"That's a possibility. So you keep your eyes open and watch for trouble. If I were them, I'd be getting my ass out of Dodge and moving to another area of the country. But these guys have egos and a score to settle."

Casey nodded to himself in the dark room. "Maybe what I ought to do is move Bertie and the kids into my house. Let these assholes know they'll be tangling with a cop."

"You can try. The thing is that these guys think they have something to prove, and they aren't going to let you, Jenn, or those kids get in their way. They got taken down because they made mistakes, but they seem to think that they can muscle their way out of them. And let me tell you, we have used everything we can think of to get them to talk, but they have all refused."

"I know. I was there for part of the interrogations, and I've never seen anything like it," Casey explained. "They all just sat there, silent." It was almost cultish.

"Anyway, we can't give them any more leverage, so keep Bertie and the kids safe, and maybe Jenn will tell us what we need to know. The chief is down everyone's neck to find these guys fast."

Casey knew that; he had already seen the bulletins. "I'll do my best," he said. He fully intended to do everything in his power to make sure that

Jolie, Beau, and Phillip, along with Bertie, stayed as safe as possible. The problem was that he didn't know how the threat would materialize. All he did know was that the sooner Jenn regained consciousness and they could talk to her to learn what she knew, the better. "I'll talk to you later."

Wyatt hung up, and Casey carried his phone upstairs and placed it beside the bed before joining Bertie under the covers. To his surprise, Smidgen jumped on the bed. "Is everything okay?" Bertie asked. "I heard you talking on the phone."

"It will be. How about we go to sleep, and I'll tell you everything in the morning." He lay down, pulling Bertie against him, cradling him in his arms as the dog pressed to the back of his legs. Then he lay still, listening for any sort of noise in the house long after Bertie's breathing had evened out and he'd fallen to sleep.

"Uncle Bertie?" Beau asked, standing in the doorway, holding his stuffie against him.

"He's asleep," Casey said softly before getting out of bed. Bertie rolled onto his side, and when Casey crouched down, Beau went right into his arms, and Casey hugged him. "What happened? Did you have a bad dream?"

Beau nodded, and Casey lifted him and took Beau back to his room, Smidgen following them. Jolie was still asleep, and Casey put Beau back in bed. "The monsters are scary."

"But I'm here, and I'm not going to let any monsters get you. I promise. I'll let you in on a secret. There are no monsters. It's just shadows and darkness. Nothing more. Your uncle Bertie and I are in the other room, and I'm big and strong and will protect you always." He made a muscle, and Beau nodded and settled under the covers. "Besides, Smidgen will be on guard if you need him." Casey scratched the dog's ears. "So go back to sleep, and I'll see you in the morning. And you and I can make special pancakes. Okay?" He kissed Beau on the forehead and quietly left the room, meeting Bertie just outside. Bertie said nothing, just took his hand and led him back to bed.

"DON'T YOU need to go to work?" Bertie asked as he took a minute from his almost frantic effort to get the kids ready to go.

"Actually, I'm off shift until tomorrow." He grinned at the kids. "I thought we could get a coffee or something before you have to open the shop." Casey began grabbing the kids' bags to carry them out to the car. "So if everyone is good, we can get a special dinner tonight." That got everyone moving much faster.

"At your house?" Beau asked.

Casey finished putting the bags in the car and scooped him up to squeals of delight. "Yes. And Smidgen can come too." He put Beau into his car seat while the others got into their places as well. "All of you have a good day today." He watched as Bertie pulled away and then went back inside and cleaned up the kitchen so Bertie wouldn't have to come home to the dishes. He also made a fresh pot of coffee.

Waiting for Bertie to return, he sat down in one of the living room chairs, and Smidgen jumped into his lap. "This isn't going to be very good." He gently stroked Smidgen's soft fur. Casey hated the fact that, in essence, they had put the kids and Bertie in danger. It hadn't been intentional. Now he wanted to move all of them out of Bertie's house to his place because he could protect them more easily, and hopefully that would put some internet search distance between them and the people who might want to use them as leverage. "The kids are just getting settled here, and I hate to move them." He looked down at the dog. "It's going to be your job to make sure they are okay."

Smidgen looked at him with those huge brown eyes like Casey was completely crazy for sitting there talking to a dog. Maybe he was.

"What are you doing?" Bertie asked, coming in from the back. "Talking to the dog?"

"He was the only one here," Casey teased as Bertie scratched the dog's head. "Look, we need to talk."

"I hate that phrase," Bertie said. "It always means bad news. I mean, no one ever says, 'Sit down, we need to talk,' and then tells you that you won a million dollars from Publishers Clearing House. Or how about we need to talk… because you *don't* have cancer." He gingerly sat down across from Casey, and Smidgen jumped to the floor and bounded onto Bertie's lap.

"I'm sorry. You didn't win a bunch of money, and you don't have cancer, as far as I know. But we do need to talk about Jenn. The police are hoping that when she wakes, they can talk to her. The two men from the flea market, well, they have everyone else intimidated into silence, and the one we had in custody is out on bail. What I want to do is bring all of you to my house for a while. It's possible that they could go after you or the kids, especially if Jenn regains consciousness. That way they can try to scare her into silence as well."

"Why were they released? These guys were distributing cocaine, pills, and maybe other stuff." Bertie seemed confused and scared.

"Our evidence against them is limited. The house belonged to one of the people we still have in custody. The people I saw packing the drugs weren't the leaders. In fact, none of us ever saw them actually doing anything. They were around, but without direct evidence against them, it's hard to pin the scheme on them. In court yesterday, their lawyer twisted things until the suspect we had was granted bail." Sometimes the system just made him angry.

"The men behind all this are out still out there, and you think they could come after the kids?" Bertie seemed highly skeptical.

"Think about it. These are two men who specialize in intimidation. The other suspects refuse to talk, and if Jenn doesn't, then they get a slap on the wrist while the others do the time. Then they'll be free to set things up all over again. How many people's lives have they wrecked already, including your sister's?" Casey asked, trying to get Bertie to understand.

"Yeah, I get that. But I can't ask these kids to move again. They're just beginning to feel a little at home here. They've already had so much change in their lives lately, and now to move them into your place, then what? For how long? Then move them back once you find these guys? And what if you don't? What if Jenn doesn't regain consciousness, or if she doesn't know anything?" Bertie continued petting Smidgen as the tension in the room rose by the second. "Am I supposed to pull them out of day care and the Y program? Then how am I supposed to do my job? Are you prepared to have guards with them all day long?" Bertie's voice grew higher as his concern grew.

Casey leaned forward to try to engage Bertie more closely. "I just want to keep you and the kids safe. That's what's truly important. It isn't going to be hard for them to find you. They know Jenn, and who knows how much she told them about her family? If they know about you, then Hodges and Wilkinson will know where you live or be able to find it. From there, they can get to you and the kids."

Bertie shook his head. "Look, I can't just uproot the kids based on supposition and fear. I know you're worried, and so am I, but what am I supposed to tell them? I can't say that they might be in danger and that bad men could come for them. Beau is already having nightmares. The others will too." Bertie paused and seemed to think. "I just can't uproot them again." Bertie closed his eyes and continued stroking Smidgen. "What can we do without doing that?" he asked quietly. "I need to keep them safe, but I can't scare them to death either."

Casey sighed. "I think we need to tell the day care that there are people who might want to get to the kids. Let them be aware. They have procedures for who can take the kids, but they should know there's a possible threat. That will allow them to be more watchful. We need to do the same with the Y program." At least he'd do what he could. Casey would much rather ensconce all four of them in his house where he could keep an eye on them, but that wasn't possible. Bertie had to work, and that meant the kids had to be watched during the day. "At night, the kids can have a sleepover at my house." He turned to Bertie. "At the store, you need to make sure you aren't alone."

"What about Jenn?"

"She's in a secure ward, and word has already been passed to those on duty to be watchful of everyone who tries to enter." He sat back. "This isn't the best way to do this, but it's what we can do."

"Then we will," Bertie said. "The kids have to have as normal a life as possible. Let them get through this without even knowing it's happening. They've already seen more than any kid should ever have to." He made a good point. This was about the three of them and how the adults in their lives could keep from scaring them half to death.

Casey paused as his phone vibrated in his pocket. He pulled it out and smiled.

"Jenn seems to be conscious," he told Bertie and responded to Wyatt's message. "I'm supposed to be off today, but I need to go up there and see if I can talk to her. You need to get to work. I'll check and see if it might be possible for all of you to see her."

"Yeah."

"And be careful. I'll follow you as far as the store to make sure you get there okay." His excitement grew. They were one step closer to wrapping this entire thing up and getting to the bottom of it all. If Jenn could fill in the missing pieces, it would be possible to get Hodges's bail revoked. From there, they might be able to find Wilkinson, and that would be the end.

Smidgen jumped down and looked up at both of them as Bertie got ready for work and let the dog out to do his business. Casey followed

Bertie to the store and made sure he got in okay before hurrying out to the hospital. He checked with the officers on duty before going into Jenn's private, secured room.

She looked like she'd been hit by a steamroller. Her eyes were puffy and dark, skin sallow and dry. At least her hair seemed to have been washed, and she'd been cleaned up.

Jenn barely turned when he came into the room. "I don't want to talk to you."

"Not even to know how your children are?" Casey asked gently as he pulled up a chair next to the bed. "I'm the one who found them after they had been alone for nearly a week and were running out of food in the house."

"Did you split them up?" she asked in a raspy voice barely louder than a whisper.

"No. They're with your brother," he reminded her in case she didn't remember. "I was able to find him, and all three are in his care." There was no need to tell her how he felt about Bertie. That wasn't pertinent to what he needed to accomplish today. "All three are doing well with Bertie and Smidgen, his dog." Casey tried to reassure her and maybe build a little trust in the process. "Smidgen seems to spend part of the night with each of the kids."

"They always wanted a dog," she said, blinking and reaching for her head. "What do you want?"

"I need to know what you do about the drug and theft operations," he told her honestly.

She rolled her head back and forth on the pillow. "They'll kill me if I talk." Her eyes grew even more haunted and hollow.

"They could go after the kids as leverage. The best way to protect your kids is to help us put the dealers out of commission. They can't get to anyone if they're put away for a long time."

Jenn turned her face toward the window, leaving the back of her head facing him. She lay that way a long time, and Casey knew he wasn't going to get anything more out of her right now. But still he had to try. "Do you want to see the kids?" Maybe it was a low blow, but she did turn back to him.

"They're better off away from me and this place," she whispered. "What good am I to them now?"

"You're still their mother, and they ask about you every day. Do you want to help them or not? Maybe since you left them alone, you really don't care." One of the machines beeped a few times, Jenn's pulse quickening for a few seconds before settling down once again. "Maybe you do."

"Of course I want to see them. They're my children, but I'm no good to them. I left, remember? I needed something more than I needed them. Do you know how that feels? To know that something is more important than the kids, but not be strong enough to do anything about it?"

"But you can do something now. You can tell me what you know. Let me put these men away for a long time. Then maybe you can have a chance to get yourself together and you can be part of your kids' lives again."

Her eyes showed the first signs of life since he'd gotten there. Casey could see traces of the same spirit Bertie had, but it seemed to be buried under a mountain of self-inflicted pain and misery.

"They'll kill me if I do," she said softly, going back to the same answer from earlier.

"And what will they do to your children if they get the chance?" Casey asked.

Once again, Jenn turned her head toward the window, and this time he didn't think he was going to get her attention back.

"You need to give it some thought. Keeping quiet is only covering up for the men who are going to leave you and the others to take the fall. I'll stop by later to talk to you again, and maybe we can arrange for you to see Beau, Jolie, and Phillip." Casey got up from the chair and left the hospital room, hoping his parting words would sink into her still drug-rattled brain.

Basically all he could hope for was that there was some sort of parental instinct still alive in her and that it was possible to reach it. The last he had seen, her eyes had returned to their blankness. Maybe the drugs had taken away so much of who she might have been that there wasn't enough of Jenn left to reach. He had seen drugs take away futures and families, stripping people down until they were just shells of who they had once been. That seemed to be what had happened to Jenn.

He left the hospital and went out to his cruiser, where he wrote up a report of his visit and got it filed before heading out. So much for his day off.

"How in the hell are we going to find these assholes?" Wyatt asked as soon as Casey contacted him through his cruiser's built-in system.

"I don't know. Hodges is out on bail."

"Yeah. But one of the terms of his bail is that he can't consort with any criminals or criminal elements. So just being with his friend Wilkinson is a violation of the parole. You know they're together. Who knows who else might be with them?" Casey had the same feeling. "I already checked out the address he gave the court, but he isn't there, and his grandmother has no idea where he is."

"He lives with his grandmother?" That was almost too much to believe. "Do you think she's part of this?"

"No. I think she's an old lady in a wheelchair who he is using to cover his tracks. She thinks he's wrongly accused and believes in his innocence." Casey could almost see Wyatt rolling his eyes. "She just smiled and said that he should be back soon… and offered me a cookie and some tea. How about you? Any luck with the mother?"

"I don't know, maybe." It was hard to tell. "I'm going to go up to try talking to her again."

"We have bulletins out for Wilkinson to every law-enforcement agency in the state, and the chief has sent out information to the local television stations. Someone is going to have seen him, and Wilkinson isn't going to be able to hide his tattoos or the way he looks for very long."

Casey received a request to come on shift through his onboard system and hung up with Wyatt, heading to the domestic disturbance call, still worried that Bertie and the kids were in danger.

THE REST of the day was as normal as any of his days got. He handled his calls, wrote reports, and called Bertie to check in a few times. At the end of his shift, he went home, straightened up, and got things ready for dinner.

"Casey, we're here," Beau called as soon as he came through the door. He raced through the house with Smidgen right behind him until Casey scooped Beau up into a hug.

"I missed you today," he said.

"Did you miss me too?" Jolie asked, and Casey set down Beau and gave her a hug too.

"I missed all three of you." He hugged Phillip as well.

Jolie snickered. "I bet you missed kissing Uncle Bertie too."

"You're such a baby," Phillip said flatly. "If they like each other, they get to kiss. It's what grown-ups do." He sat in one of the chairs and fished his iPad out of his bag.

"I got to see your mom today. She's awake and doing better. Maybe I can take you up to see her in a few days." He hoped that would be good news for the kids.

"Your mom is still pretty sick, so we need to send her get-well thoughts," Bertie cautioned, but the kids were all excited.

"But your mom said to tell you all hello and that she's thinking about you," Casey added as the kids all looked at him with something that resembled hope. The exception was Phillip, who seemed skeptical and went into the other room without a word. Casey shared a brief look with Bertie, who sighed.

"How was work otherwise?" Bertie asked, and Casey took a second to kiss him, regardless of the giggles from their audience.

"Difficult," Casey answered softly. "I'll tell you more later." The longer Hodges and Wilkinson were out there, the more his concern grew. He had no illusions that Wilkinson was going to pay any attention to the terms of Hodges's bail when it came to intimidation and keeping himself out of jail.

"Can we go play with Smidgen out back?" Jolie asked.

"Yes. But don't trample Casey's plants, okay?" Bertie answered and let them out into the fenced-in yard. "Phillip, do you want to go outside too?" He got up and followed the other kids.

"I'm really concerned for him. He should be able to laugh and have fun, except he's so quiet, and it worries me," Bertie said.

"You have every right to be worried, and so does he. When I saw Jenn, she was pretty absorbed with herself. I did ask her about the kids, and she said they were better off without her. I think she wants to see them, and she does care for them, but she's scared to death that the dealers will kill her if she talks. I'm wondering what we missed."

Bertie tilted his head to the side. "I don't understand."

"The show of power. If everyone is so afraid, it has to be more than threats. There has to have been some demonstration that terrorized these people into silence. Maybe you and I need to go see Jenn together, because she might talk to you. She's scared, but if these men did something to scare so many people into silence, then we need to know what it is. Your sister must know. And someone who would do that will definitely make a second strength move to keep up the pressure."

"Will they let me in to see her?" Bertie asked. "All I want is for this to be over so Jenn can start to heal and we can figure out some sort of future." He lifted his gaze. "I just wish I knew what that looked like."

Casey tugged Bertie into a hug. "Whatever it is, I know I'm not letting you go." He had no intention of walking away like he had all those years ago.

"Even if being part of my life means three kids and a dog too?" Bertie asked roughly.

Casey drew closer. "I love those kids, that dog, and I love you too. So yeah, however our future looks, I'm here with you." He gently wound his arms around Bertie's neck, drawing him in for a kiss that threatened to steam up all the windows. Casey had no idea what any sort of future with Bertie would look like, but that was okay, as long as there *was* a future.

CHAPTER 10

"I THINK I get it now," Casey said gently once the kids were in bed. Bertie checked the back door to ensure it was locked.

"And what is that?" Bertie asked, turning out the kitchen light. Somehow almost every light in the house ended up on. He even opened the door and peered into the basement to make sure those lights were off.

"The kids think of your house as home." Casey slipped his arms around Bertie's waist, and Bertie leaned back into the embrace. He closed his eyes and let the feelings of comfort and safety overtake him. In Casey's arms, he knew things were going to be okay. It was other times he worried. "They got tired, and Beau climbed in my lap, leaning against my chest, and said he was ready to go home. He didn't mean Jenn's house, but this one." He squeezed a little tighter. "I just wish...."

"I know. The cop in you wants to make sure that we're all safe. But we can't be encased in bubble wrap. We'll do what we can and keep our eyes open. If someone is intent on trying to get to us, I don't think which house we're staying at is going to make much of a difference." Bertie tried to let go of the anxiety that had taken root when Casey told him the situation. He'd wanted to yell about how they could let someone like Hodges out on bail. But that wasn't going to do any damned good.

"Keeping you safe is more than just a cop thing." He brushed his hand over Bertie's cheek. "I'll do what I can to protect my family."

Bertie swallowed hard around the lump in his throat and closed his eyes.

"I know you're worried, but I'll stand in front of the world for all of you."

Bertie hugged Casey, resting his head against his shoulder. "Let's hope it doesn't come to that."

"Yeah," Casey whispered before following Bertie up to bed.

"ARE WE really going to see Mommy?" Jolie asked as Bertie got them ready to go. It was all quite a production, but this time more than usual because he had insisted that they dress in their best clothes to look nice for Jenn. Phillip seemed skeptical, but in the end, he'd done what Bertie had asked.

"Yes, we are," Bertie said with a sense of excitement mixed with dread. He hoped he hid the worried part well enough that the kids didn't pick up on it.

"Is Casey coming too?" Beau asked, tugging at the collar of his shirt. He stopped when Bertie gave him a stern look.

"He's at work, but he's going to meet us at the hospital in a little while." Bertie tried to stay calm. Looking the kids over, he smiled and ushered them out of the house and to the car. They climbed into their places, and he made sure they were all buckled in. Maybe he should get a bigger car so Phillip could have more room. "You all ready?" He tried to muster some excitement as he pulled away from the curb, heading through late-afternoon Carlisle traffic and out to the hospital on the west side of town.

He parked relatively close to the front door and followed the directions Casey had given him up to the ward where Jenn had her room.

"Excuse me," he said to the officer outside the secure area. "I was told by Trooper Bombaro that we could see Jenn Riley. These are her children, and he said he had cleared the visit." Bertie forced his mind to work, not knowing what kind of shape she was going to be in. The two youngest held each of his hands, and they fidgeted with their own nerves.

"The visit is cleared, but there has to be someone with you. Just a minute." He made a radio call and received an answer almost immediately. "He's just pulling into the lot and will be right up."

Bertie let go of Jolie and lifted Beau into his arms.

"Will Mommy remember us?" Beau asked softly, resting his head on Bertie's shoulder. God, that question about broke Bertie's heart. He wasn't able to talk right away and found the other two looking up at him, waiting for an answer.

"Of course she will," he answered softly, his throat aching. He held Jolie's hand while Phillip looked around, almost pressed to his side.

Finally Casey strode down the hall in full uniform. For a second Bertie's heart sped up at the sight. He was sexy as hell dressed like that, and Bertie let that wash over him. It was better than the sense of impending dread that returned moments later.

"Hey, guys," Casey said cheerfully. "Are you ready to go see your mom?" He thanked the trooper and then opened the door and led them down a short hallway before pausing outside Jenn's room. "You go on in to see her." He came closer to Bertie. "Remember that Jenn is under arrest. Don't talk about what happened or try to get her to confess to anything. Just talk to her like a brother, okay?" He spoke very softly.

Bertie nodded. He had no intention of going over past events. It was best if the kids had a good visit with her. That was all that counted in his book. "Remember that we need to be quiet, so use your inside voices."

He led the way into the room, still carrying Beau, who buried his face in his neck once they entered the room. "Hi, Jenn," he said gently, pulling her attention away from the window.

"Mommy," Jolie said, hurrying to the bed.

Jenn moved slowly but eventually took her hand. "Hi, sweetheart," she said in little more than a whisper. Her eyes seemed blank, and she moved like she was in water, in a sort of exaggerated slow motion. "My pretty girl." She patted Jolie's head and extended her hand to Phillip, who slowly took it.

"Hi, Mom," he said, but he stayed where he was and pressed closer to Bertie. Jenn was going to have to work to win back her oldest son. "Are you feeling better?"

"My head is fuzzy, and I don't remember things very well. But I remember all of you." She half smiled at Beau, who squirmed, and Bertie placed him on the side of the bed. He lay down next to her, and thankfully Jenn put an arm around him. "Are you all being good?"

"I made you a picture. Uncle Bertie got us crayons and markers and all kinds of stuff." Jolie held up the picture, and Jenn took it, brought it closer, then handed it back.

"It's beautiful. Can you put it on the bulletin board so I can see it when I'm awake?" Bertie placed it along the side of the board and tucked it in so it would stay since there were no pins to tack it up—nothing that could possibly be used as a weapon. "Thank you."

"Mommy, when are you coming home?" Jolie asked.

"It will be a while," Jenn said. "The three of you need to be good for your uncle Bertie." She held out her hand, and Bertie took it. She squeezed slightly and left it there. Her eyes began to close, and Bertie wondered how long they should stay. She seemed worn out already.

"We can visit again," Bertie said gently, and he helped Beau down off the bed. "Say goodbye for now." Each of the kids said their goodbyes before leaving the room. Bertie turned to where Casey stood with them, ready to go himself, but Jenn held his hand.

"Please take care of them," she said softly. "I… I messed up bad, and my head is wrong. I can't think and I can't really remember. Just take care of them and give the kids a good life." A tear ran down her cheek.

"Jenn," Bertie said, his throat aching.

"No. I was never a good mother. I left my kids alone. That part I remember. The drugs made me feel better, and…." She released his hand. "Just promise me that you'll care for them and love them. That's all I ask."

"Of course I will," Bertie said. "You know I will."

"Then forget about me. Just go and help them to forget. It's better that way. Give them the life they deserve. The one they could never have if they were with me." Her gaze met his, and her eyes seemed clear all of a sudden. "No matter what, make sure they have a good life. I put the drugs and what I wanted ahead of them. And now I can't remember my babies being born. It's all a blur. I traded them away." She sniffed and wiped her eyes. "I traded everything away."

"Jenn," Bertie said, pulling up the chair. "You need to concentrate on getting better, and you need to tell the police whatever you know. Help them end this, please." He squeezed her hand. "The guys know that you have kids. What if they try to hurt them?"

"They'll kill me," she whispered and then let out a sigh that seemed to rattle in her chest. "What does it matter? Maybe I'm better off dead."

"What did they do to scare you so badly?" Bertie asked. "Was it Hodges or Wilkinson?"

Jenn closed her eyes, shuddering hard enough to make the bed vibrate. "Wilkinson. David was always the mean one. He made sure we all knew what would happen if we said a word." She whined softly. "He used a rabbit, and he…." She turned away, shoulders shaking. "This I remember. He…. The poor thing…." She continued crying. "He did it more than once so everyone would get the idea that he liked hurting it." She slowly rolled her head back. "Tell that cop friend of yours to come in. I'll tell him whatever he wants to know."

"Thank you," Bertie said softly.

"I'll do it for my kids. I owe it to them. Just make sure they don't ever find out how bad I got. When you tell them stories about me, be sure to tell them the good parts."

Bertie leaned closer. "How about we make a deal? You get better, and when you're able, you and I will tell them all about the things we did when we were kids. We'll share our stories, and you can spend some time with them. Okay?" What Jenn said sounded way too much like goodbye. "I know things are tough right now, but they will get better. I promise you that." He squeezed her hand once more and then went out into the hallway.

"Let's go down and see if we can find a snack," Bertie told the kids before leaning close to Casey. "Go in there now. She'll tell you what you want to know." He took the kids' hands and led them away, leaving Casey behind to do his job.

"Is Mom going to be sick forever?" Phillip asked once Bertie had gotten drinks for everyone and seated them at a table with a couple orders of french fries.

"We'll have to wait and see how she does. Your mom is pretty sick right now. But all three of you are going to stay with me. I'm thinking that this weekend we can go look at bunk beds for Beau and Jolie. I thought that we could get some things to make your room more comfortable. We'll also go back to the house and get all your stuff." He might as well make the kids as comfortable and as happy as possible. "What do you think?"

Phillip nodded. "Can I get stuff that I like?"

"What about what's at your mom's house?"

"It was there when we moved in." He looked down at the floor. "Mom said it was the best she could do."

"We'll make you up a nice room," Bertie said. "And we'll work together to pick out the things for it."

Phillip actually smiled and then started eating. The others grinned at each other, dipping their fries in ketchup. By the time the kids were slurping the last of their drinks, Casey hurried into the room.

"I need to go to the station right away and file my report," he whispered to him.

Bertie nodded. He understood that whatever Casey had found out was important.

"Are you ready to go?" Bertie asked the kids. "Let's throw away the trash, and then we can go out to the car." He helped the kids take care of things while Casey spoke softly on the phone. "We'll see you at the house when you're done." He patted Casey's arm and then led the kids to the hospital exit.

The sun had set while they were inside, and he hurried them across the patchily lighted parking lot to the car.

"Where do you think you're going in such a hurry?"

Bertie turned just as the man with the bobcat tattoo on his neck came down the aisle of parked cars.

"Get behind me," Bertie told the kids, stepping in front to try to protect them. "Where's your friend?" Bertie had a suspicion that he wasn't alone and tried to see where the other mastermind of this miserable situation could be.

"Oh, he's around." The sneer was unsettling. "I want all of you to walk forward slowly and stay together. We're going to go for a little ride." He pulled a gun from his pocket to help make his point. Beau began to cry, along with Jolie. Phillip stayed close, holding the other two's hands, while Bertie stayed in front, hoping to hell his knees didn't give out. He was scared to death, but there was no way in hell this asshole was going to take his kids anywhere.

"No one is going anywhere," Bertie said as calmly as he could.

"Yes, you are. You all are. Their spaced-out mother will keep her mouth shut once she knows we have her kids. She'll clam up tight, and that will give us a chance to get away."

"Too late. Jenn has already talked to the police, and they have everything they need. Your only chance is to get the hell out of here and put as much distance between you and them as possible. It's your one opportunity, as slim as it is." Bertie took another step forward, trying to intimidate him. The doors to the hospital were only a little ways back.

"Kids, run," he said. "You run back inside and scream for help. Go! Fast as you can!" Bertie stood his ground, seeing Phillip in his peripheral vision lift Beau and take Jolie's hand, taking off across the parking lot. "You're going to have to go through me to get to them." He spoke loudly. "That's right. You can shoot me, you motherfucker, but those kids are off-limits to an asshole like you."

A shot rang out, and Bertie took a step back, expecting the roar of pain, but nothing happened. Maybe he was already dead.

The other man's eyes grew wide, and then he collapsed onto the pavement as Casey hurried up to him. People raced out of the hospital.

"I need medical help for this man right away!" Casey shouted. "This man has been shot." He kicked the man's gun away and was already putting pressure on the wound as medical professionals raced out and took over. "He's a suspect and is under arrest," he told them. "Additional units are on the way." Casey then read the man his rights.

Bertie's knees felt like Jell-O, but he managed to stay upright until Casey helped him sit down on the ground. "Don't you ever do that again. My heart nearly stopped when I saw you staring down a guy with a gun."

"The kids. All I could think about was getting them away." He looked around. "Where are they?"

"Inside with one of the nurses. She got them settled down as I was coming out." His panting sounded like Casey had run a marathon. "God, don't do that to me again."

"I won't," Bertie promised as sirens sounded in the distance. They grew closer, and eventually police units made the turn into the hospital.

For the next hour it was a million questions from all sides, even for Casey. Mostly, Bertie sat with the kids, trying to answer their questions as well and holding them, their fear and its release giving Bertie some direction. It didn't matter what he felt at the moment. He had to make sure Beau, Jolie, and Phillip were okay.

"Can we go now?" Bertie asked as Wyatt approached.

"Yes. We have all your statements, as well as the ones from people inside the hospital. Casey is going to be buried in paperwork until IA reviews his use of his firearm. It seems fully justified, but it's standard procedure."

"Okay. Then I'm going to take them home. What about the other man?"

Wyatt grinned. "Your sister was able to give us a few places to look, and a team found him at his grandmother's, hiding in a pantry cellar in the basement a few minutes ago. And now that we have them all, as well as your sister's statement, the others are starting to talk as well."

"Is it all over?" Phillip asked.

Wyatt nodded. "It's over," he said with a smile. "You all go home with your uncle Bertie. And by the way, guys...." Wyatt knelt down. "He's a real hero. And so were all of you for listening to him and running away as fast as you did. That was really brave."

Bertie had never been so relieved in his life. It was over. They had found Jenn, and the people who had helped ruin her life were in custody. That didn't change whatever consequences Jenn was going to have to face, but that would come in time. The really important thing was that the kids were safe and in one piece.

He turned to where Casey stood with the other troopers and officers, his gut clenching. All of this was over, and everything was going to change now.

For the past couple of weeks, he and Casey had pretty much been in each other's pockets. Casey had helped him with the kids and had ensured that they were safe. Now that the situation had changed, Bertie knew that things would be different between him and Casey. He just didn't know how. Regardless of what Casey said, it was a lot to expect that he would be willing to step into Bertie's life now that he was going to have the kids long-term.

"Can we go home now?" Beau asked.

Bertie forced a smile for their sakes. "Yes. I'll make you some dinner, and then once you have your jammies on, I'll tell you all stories about me and your mom when we were growing up." No, things were never going to be the same again—not for him, the kids, or Jenn. But he could concentrate on the good for their sakes. The rest they could deal with in time.

"DID MOMMY really do that?" Jolie asked.

"Yup. She was just your age when she got her first bicycle. She wanted a pink one, and she got right on and started riding. She was really amazing." Bertie smiled and looked out the front window again. Casey had said that he'd be over, and every noise made Bertie jumpy. He'd had no messages, and he wondered if Casey had changed his mind… about everything.

"I have a bicycle. It's at Mommy's," Jolie said.

"Then we'll go get it, along with your other things. Do you know how to ride?" Bertie asked.

"Not yet. The road was too busy," Phillip chimed in.

"Then we'll go to the park, and you can both bring your bikes. And you…." Bertie tickled Beau. "We'll get you one too." Bertie was worn out, but thankfully the kids were winding down too. "Let's get you all in bed." He took their hands, leading them upstairs.

THE KIDS were asleep and the house was quiet. Bertie had his phone nearby as he watched television in the living room. He kept checking outside, but still hadn't heard anything from Casey. Maybe he was being stupid to think that Casey had really wanted to be part of their lives. He had said so, but now Bertie wasn't so sure. God, he hated being this damned insecure. It was only a few hours, and Casey was most likely at work, wrapping up all the details of his investigation. Still, it was strange that Casey hadn't even messaged. But then… things had changed.

He was sure that Casey cared for him and the kids, but maybe that was all due to some sort of protective instinct from being a police officer. The more he sat and thought, the more he wondered and then hated himself for it. He was being stupid and just needed to go up to bed.

Bertie made sure the doors were locked and turned out the lights. He was climbing the stairs when a soft knock sounded on the front door. Bertie retraced his steps and peered out the side window before opening the door. "I thought that…," he began, a little ashamed for his worry now that Casey stood in front of him.

"My personal phone died because I was on it so much. I probably should have just emailed you, but things have been chaotic." Casey closed the door before pulling Bertie into hug.

Bertie wound his arms around Casey's neck and humphed when he was pushed back against the door, the panels pressing into his back. The kiss swept Bertie off his feet, and he went with it, winding his legs around Casey's waist.

"You looked worried when you answered the door," Casey whispered and kissed him again.

"I was being stupid," he whispered back.

"Somehow I doubt that," Casey retorted and then paused, listening. "Are the kids asleep?"

Bertie nodded, his breath mingling with Casey's, the heat wisping over his cheeks. "They were so excited from seeing their mom that it wore them out, and they dropped off a few hours ago."

"Good." Casey placed his hands under Bertie's butt and carried him up the stairs.

"What are you doing?"

"Taking the man I love to bed," Casey growled softly, and just like that, Bertie's worries melted away, instantly replaced with near blinding desire. "I want you, Bertie, in my life and in my bed… your bed…." He lightly kicked the bedroom door closed behind them. "Doesn't matter which one." He smirked. "Though my bed is bigger, and so is the house," he added slyly.

"How about we give things a little time before you and I shack up?" Bertie couldn't help smiling. "Give the kids some time. Then we can ask them what they want too." He already knew what he wanted, and it involved this man, years—*decades*—a big family….

Casey smiled as he laid Bertie back on the mattress without a word, then pulled off his clothes until Bertie lay naked on the bedding. "I can live with that. What I can't live without is you." He leaned closer. "I always knew you had the biggest heart of anyone I ever met, but you're a tiger as well."

Bertie play-scratched at Casey's chest, then groaned as he moved away. Casey got out of his clothes quickly, with Bertie enjoying the view. Then he was back, leaning over him, pressing Bertie into the mattress. The energy between them spiked within seconds, Casey sending shivers of pleasure racing through Bertie, threatening to break out, but Bertie kept quiet, holding all of it inside, letting it build as Casey caressed him, tasted him, and then, with enough power to nearly make his head explode, entered him, joining the two of them together, heart, body, and soul. Bertie could feel it all, every movement, even the beat of Casey's heart. Their souls linked through their eyes, and they held each other, enthralled, as their bodies moved as one. There were moments when Bertie lost himself not in Casey, but in the two of them. Like magic, their coupling transported him, leaving him sated and wishing for more… so much more. *Years* of more.

"I love you," Bertie whispered as Casey held him, sleep already seeming to want to overtake him. "I think I always have."

"And I love you," Casey whispered. The words hung in the air like the perfect cloud.

Bertie rolled over, facing Casey, and slowly scooted closer.

Casey slipped his arms around him. "It was a weird road that led me back to you—that gave us a second chance."

Bertie lifted his head off the pillow. "Are you disappointed? You couldn't have imagined that it would come with so many complications."

Casey hugged him, tugging Bertie until he lay on top of Casey, staring into his eyes. "I'm not disappointed, and I wouldn't change how things worked out. I love you and our entire family." He kissed Bertie hard.

"But what if—"

"No buts. We'll handle the future as it comes. As long as you're part of it, that's all that matters."

Bertie couldn't argue with that.

EPILOGUE

BERTIE HELD his breath as he opened the oven and pulled out the turkey. It was his first attempt at roasting the whole bird, and the scent wafted through Casey's kitchen.

"Is it time to eat?" Beau asked. He had turned five a month ago and was growing like a weed. All of the kids seemed happy and smiled a lot. The anxiety that had permeated them when they'd first come to him seemed a thing of the past.

"When will Uncle Casey and Mommy get here?" Jolie asked.

"In a few minutes. Why don't you help your brother set the table so we can eat right when they arrive?" He set the pan on a hot pad and checked carefully that the turkey was done.

Casey had arranged for Jenn to come to Thanksgiving for a few hours. She had been placed in a facility that would allow her to get the treatment and help she needed for her mental illness. The judge had ruled her incapacitated and ordered help for her rather than simply jail time. She was to be evaluated regularly to gauge her improvement.

Unfortunately, as far as Bertie could see, there had been very little. What the drugs hadn't taken from her left a sketchy shell of the person he remembered. Still, Bertie went to see her regularly and made sure she had money in her account for anything she might need.

"She's here!" Jolie cried over a clang of silverware, and then she ran through the house to the front door, pulling it open as Casey and Jenn came inside.

"Hi, sweetheart," Jenn said slowly, her words measured like she wanted to make sure they were right.

Beau hurried through as well and got a hug and a smile from his mom. Phillip stayed in the dining room, keeping his distance.

Bertie joined him. "Go say hi to your mom," he said gently, and knelt down when Phillip hesitated. "You need to forgive her if you can," he said gently. "I know it's hard, but try. Your mom is ill and probably always will be, but that doesn't mean she doesn't love you." He held out his arms, and Phillip went right into them, his shoulders shaking.

"I don't want to be bad like her," Phillip whispered as he buried his head against Bertie's shoulder.

"You won't be," he whispered. "You'll be Phillip, and you'll make your own mistakes and have your own triumphs. But no matter what, we'll love you. We always will. And so will she." He backed away. "I know it can be hard sometimes, but we have to take a person for who they are."

"But my mom is…." He didn't say the word as Bertie frowned.

"She needs help, and she's getting it." He stood back up. "Remember when you helped save Beau and Jolie? You were brave. Letting go of hurt and forgiving people is also brave." He ruffled Phillip's hair, and he nodded, setting down the last of the silverware.

Bertie put the remaining silverware at each place, watching through the archway to the other room where Phillip said hello to his mom.

Jenn smiled and said something, holding out her arms, and Bertie turned away as Phillip went to her, Smidgen nearby, wagging his tail. Bertie called him, and the dog hurried over. "You need to be good, and no begging." He smiled and then returned to the kitchen to get dinner on the table.

"Do you need help?" Casey asked as he came in.

"Don't you need to stay with her?" Casey had explained that Jenn was here under his supervision and that he was responsible for her.

"Phillip asked to talk to her, so I thought it best to give her and the kids a few minutes." Still, Bertie peeked back out the doorway and through to the living room, where Jenn sat on the sofa with Beau on Phillip's lap and Jolie on the other side of her.

"You could mash the potatoes while I carve the turkey, and then we can bring in the rest." He got busy, and soon he and Casey carried in turkey, potatoes, the cranberry sauce, gravy, beans, and a salad. The table practically groaned under the weight of the food.

Bertie called everyone in, and they took their places, with Jenn moving slowly. She sat next to Casey for one of the best family Thanksgiving meals he could remember in a long time.

"I have something I'd like to say," Casey said once dinner was done and before dessert had been brought out. "You know that Bertie and I have been seeing each other for some time now."

"Are you going to get married?" Jolie asked with a grin.

Casey put his hand over his heart and turned to Bertie. "She stole my thunder," he said gently and pulled a small box out of his pocket. "See, yes. I want to ask your uncle Bertie to marry me, but I wanted to know if it was okay with you…." He turned to each of the kids, and Jenn as well, who nodded and smiled.

Bertie could hardly breathe, looking at Casey.

"Yes," Jolie said, bouncing in her chair, grinning from ear to ear. "Can I be flower girl?"

"Yay," Beau cried, just as excited as could be.

Phillip smiled. "Of course." He was growing up so fast and trying to act mature.

Casey turned back to Bertie, gaze soft, gentle, and intense enough to make Bertie shake.

"I let you go once, and I'm not going to do it again. Will you marry me?" Casey asked, and Bertie nodded, trying to find his voice.

"Yes," Bertie said, barely able to speak, he was so choked up. "I'll marry you, and we can all be a family."

Casey pulled him into a hug, Smidgen barked, and the kids cheered as they hurried over, joining in the family hug.

Keep reading for an excerpt from
Rekindled Flame
by Andrew Grey.

THE ROAR and screech of the siren faded into the background as the truck slowed to a stop. Morgan popped his seat belt off and jumped down as the wheels quit rolling. Seconds mattered. He'd had that drilled into him since his first day of training, and it was now ingrained into his base personality. He was already pulling hoses off the back of the truck, laying them out as others hooked them up without a word. They knew exactly what to do. They'd practiced so many times they did their jobs without thinking about it.

"The upper floor is nearly completely engulfed. Get some water on it right away," the captain said even as the hose was connected and pressure began to build inside it.

Morgan turned to the group of people gathered in sleepwear toward the back of the lawn, huddled together. He hurried over as soon as the sound of water and fire mixing sent a hiss of steam into the air. "Is everyone out?" he asked them. They looked at each other, stunned.

"Richard isn't here," a kid in blue pajamas answered after a few seconds.

"Oh God," the woman, presumably the mother, groaned. "He lives in the small apartment." She pointed to the side addition of the compact house. "The door is right around the side."

"Thanks, ma'am," Morgan said and hurried back to the captain. "Someone is still inside. The family hasn't seen the tenant, Richard. I'm getting my breathing gear." He didn't wait for an answer as he pulled on a tank and mask with practiced ease. Time was of the essence. Even with the water that was being poured on the structure, the fire was still hot and doing its best to consume the old, dry home. He had a few seconds to ponder just why the house was going up so quickly before he was hurrying up the yard, water running down his suit to give him an initial layer of protection before he went in.

"Shit," he said into his communication system. "There's a ramp." He kicked open the side door. Blinding smoke poured out. Morgan hesitated for a second to give the worst of it the chance to escape before plunging into a world of danger.

The fire roared continually, even though he couldn't see it. The air was hot and getting hotter, which told him the fire was just on the other side of the walls and would most likely break through at any second. He scanned the small living area and then opened the first door he saw. It was empty of anyone as far as he could see. Morgan turned and pushed at another door. It didn't move. Without hesitating, he kicked it, sending the door flying inward.

A man sat in a wheelchair, slumped forward. Morgan had no time to assess his condition. The air was smoky and getting worse.

A crash sounded behind him, and the heat increased. Lights now danced on the walls of the other room. Morgan hefted the man into his arms and over his shoulder. Then he turned and left the room.

Flames crawled across the ceiling, heading for the same door as Morgan. It was a race: him to the exit and the fire to the source of air. Morgan walked as quickly as he could carrying the weight, the flames now racing throughout the room. He knew that within seconds his exit would be closed off.

A figure appeared in the doorway, and water shot to the side and above him, buying Morgan precious seconds that he was able to use to reach the door and safety. He stepped outside and down the ramp, heading right for the first ambulance he saw.

EMTs met him in the yard with a stretcher, and he laid Richard down on it as gently as he could and stepped back, hoping like hell he wasn't too late. Morgan took off his helmet and breathed, taking in cool, clear air. He was sweating like a pig and pulled open the latches of his fire coat to let some of the spring air inside. A bottle of water was shoved into his hand, and he drank without thinking, looking to where he'd left Richard and sighing with relief when he saw him with a breathing mask on. No CPR, just oxygen. He was breathing.

"You did good, again," the captain said, motioning him away from the others. "But this breakneck decision-making of yours has to stop," he added softly. "You ran in there before anyone could assess the situation." A crash interrupted them as the front wall of the home collapsed and fell inward. "You could have been inside."

"So could that man. Instead we're both outside and safe." He and the captain didn't see eye to eye on a number of things, least of which was the speed Morgan thought things needed to be done. The captain was too cautious and lost precious time, in his opinion. But he kept that to himself for now. "You know seconds count. We've all been taught that from day one. I used those seconds to rescue a man in a wheelchair." There was no way the captain could argue with that result.

"All right. It worked out this time, but what if you'd been caught inside?" he countered.

Morgan nodded and went back to work. Having an argument now wasn't going to get him anything, and the captain was worked up enough that if he pressed it, Morgan would find himself in front of the chief once again to explain why he'd done the right thing. It was getting annoying.

He went over to where the EMTs were loading Richard into the back of the ambulance. "Is he going to be all right?"

"He got way too much smoke, but we believe you got to him in time. He's already breathing somewhat better, and he's starting to come around, but he's still groggy and out of it. We're transporting him, but I suspect you saved his life."

"Thanks, Gary." Over time he'd gotten to know most of the ambulance drivers and EMTs. It was a hazard of the profession that their paths crossed too many times. They shook hands, and Morgan turned and went back to where the rest of the guys continued to pour water on what was left of the house, dousing the last of the flames.

By the time they started packing up, the Red Cross had arrived and was meeting with the family. Jackets had been provided, as had water and something to eat. Morgan knew from experience that they'd be helped with temporary shelter as well as given guidance for wading through dealing with insurance and trying to rebuild their lives.

Morgan walked to where they stood.

"Is Richard going to be okay?" the same young boy asked.

"We think so. They're going to take him to the hospital. Is he a family member?" Morgan asked.

"Sort of," the woman said. "He was in the same unit as my brother, Billy, and has been renting the apartment for the last year or so. The kids adore him and call him Uncle Rich, but he isn't a blood relation."

"Billy didn't make it home," the man standing with her explained, and Morgan nodded.

"He'll most likely be taken to Harrisburg Hospital. It's the closest, and they'll do everything they can for him. For now, get yourselves somewhere safe and warm for the night." The kids had to be getting cold in the night air, and he had work he had to do to help the other guys clean up. At times like this, he was never sure what to say, so he tipped his hat and joined the men draining the hoses to load them back on the trucks.

"That was something else," Henry Porter said, smile shining on his smoke-smudged face. "When I saw you coming out of that smoke, it was a damn miracle."

"You got there just in time," Morgan told the younger firefighter, returning his smile. "I wasn't certain I was going to make it until you bought me the time."

"You were going to make it, but I was glad to help." He was all smiles as they rolled up the hoses.

"I heard the guy was a veteran," Jimmy Connors said, gathering the nozzles and other equipment. "In a wheelchair."

"Apparently," Morgan said. "It was a good night. Everyone got out." He hated seeing the faces of families who had lost everything. They always seemed so haunted and unsure of what was going to happen next. Morgan had seen that in the family tonight, along with relief that Richard had been rescued safely.

"All right, let's get the last of this packed up so we can go back to the station," the captain called encouragingly, and their talking ceased as they all got to work. What could be pulled out and put to use in a matter of minutes always took much longer to stow and get ready for the next time it was needed. When the equipment was stowed and the area cleaned up, they climbed into the trucks and quietly went back to the station.

Morgan dragged himself off the truck. The energy that had sustained him at the fire and through the rescue had now deserted him, and all he wanted was to climb into a bed. Working late when most people are asleep was the hardest part of this job for him. Morgan was a morning person. At home he was usually up early, always had been, so working late into the night went counter to his natural rhythm.

"Let's get the hoses set to dry and call it a night. The rest can wait," the captain said, and the men got to work and then headed inside and up to the dormitory. They often worked long shifts, and catching a few hours' sleep was always a godsend. Some of the guys would sit at the table and play cards or talk through the entire shift. Not Morgan. He headed right up and took his turn in the bathroom, then collapsed on one of the narrow beds, letting oblivion take over for a little while.

He only slept for a few hours, just long enough to recharge his batteries, and then he was up once again, helping to prepare the equipment for the next call, which they all knew could come at any moment.

"What will you do now that your rotation is over and you have some time off?" Henry asked without looking up from where he was cleaning the side of the pumper. The younger man's enthusiasm always seemed to run over the brim.

"I don't know. Probably sleep for a while, and then…." That was always the part of that answer that vexed him. Outside of work he didn't have much of a life.

"Will you go out, find someone to keep you company?" Henry waggled his eyebrows and reminded Morgan just how young Henry was and how old he seemed to be getting. "There are some great clubs downtown, and the girls would be more than interested, if you know what I mean. They love firemen."

"Is that why you became one?" Morgan asked. He was only giving Henry a hard time. Being a firefighter had to be in your blood or you didn't last very long. The job demanded a lot, physically, personally. It tended to take over and become what your life—well, at least his life— revolved around. Relationships suffered, and most went by the wayside over time.

"You know it's not," Henry answered seriously. "But it is one of the perks of the job."

Morgan paused. "You know you aren't likely to see me in one of those particular clubs." Morgan had decided some years earlier that he wasn't going to hide who he was.

"I thought that was only rumor and such." Henry looked him over. "You don't look like you're… that way." From what Henry had said and the way he'd talked sometimes, Morgan figured Henry had come to them straight off a rural Lancaster farm.

"Gay people come in all shapes and sizes, and believe it or not, we can do just about anything."

Henry's gaze drifted to the floor, hand stopping for a second. "I didn't mean anything by it. I guess you're just the first gay person I've met." He continued working.

"I don't think so. You remember Angus, the man who came in at the last training session talking about how fires start? He has a partner who isn't a woman. They've been together about a year now, I guess. His name's Kevin, and he's really nice."

"You know them?"

"I've met Kevin one time." Morgan didn't want to go into how all gay people didn't necessarily know each other. It wasn't his job to educate the kid, nor was it wise to try to pop too many of his bubbles all at once. "You okay?"

"Yeah," Henry answered quickly.

Morgan knew he was covering some discomfort, and Morgan figured that was okay. "If you've got questions, ask."

Henry wiped faster and faster. Soon Morgan figured either his arm was going to fall off or he was going to rub right through the red paint.

"There's no reason to be upset or nervous."

He finally stopped and set down the rag, working his arm in a circle because he must have made it sore. "But what if…." He stopped and shook his head. "I'm being dumb, right?"

"Maybe a little?" Morgan teased. "Now get back to work, and try not to rub all the paint off." He picked up another rag and helped the kid. Polishing was one of the most detailed and mind-numbing jobs, and usually it fell to the newbies. Morgan never minded it, and he could help the kid out. They were all a team.

Once his shift was over a few hours later, Morgan gathered his things to get ready to leave. There had been no further calls, and turnover to the morning shift had been completed. "You working today too?" Morgan asked Henry when he didn't seem to be getting ready to go.

"They're a man short, and I volunteered. They need the help, and I can use the hours."

"Don't wear yourself out. This job is a marathon that can last a long time." He clapped the young firefighter on the shoulder.

"Don't worry," Phillips, one of the senior firefighters, said. "We'll make sure he gets rest."

Morgan nodded and hefted his bag. "Are you going somewhere in particular?" Henry asked, following him out.

"Yeah, I'm going to stop at the hospital to see how the man I helped last night is doing, and then I'm going home." Morgan headed for the door and threw his bag into the trunk of his car before pulling out and driving across town to a place he knew way too well.

Morgan had saved a number of people over the years. It was one of the things that went with the job. Not getting there in time could rip a firefighter apart, and saving someone brought you a kinship no one else could understand. All he knew about this man was that his name was Richard, but in a few minutes they had shared something unique. Morgan had had an influence on the rest of Richard's life.

"Can I help you?" the woman behind the visitors' desk asked as he approached. "Oh, hi, Morgan," she said when she recognized him. "What can I do for you?"

"There was a man brought into emergency last night. His first name was Richard. I need to know what room he's in."

"You don't want much," she told him and began typing. Geri was used to his unorthodox inquiries. She was a little younger than him and had worked at the hospital for years. "What happened to him?"

"I got him out of a burning building last night, and I want to make sure he's okay." He leaned against the counter, relaxing while she searched.

"I found him. Room 212. It says he can receive visitors."

She handed him a pass, and Morgan thanked her before striding toward the elevators. He rode to the second floor and then walked through familiar hallways to the ward and down to Richard's room. He paused outside and heard nothing. Peering in, he saw a sleeping figure in the bed. Maybe he'd come too early. He walked in anyway and stood by the end of the bed.

"Who are you?" Richard demanded in a rough voice that set Morgan on alert.

"I'm the firefighter who pulled you out last night. I just wanted to make sure you were okay."

"You rescued me from the fire?" he asked. "You should have saved your efforts and left me there. Everyone would be so much better off." The anger and vitriol rolled off him in a tidal wave of blackness.

"Well, I did," Morgan said as he put his jacket on the nearby chair. "The kids were worried about you."

That softened some of Richard's features as a nurse came rushing into the room. "Mr. Smalley, you need to remain calm." She helped him to lie back down, glaring at Morgan. "His breathing needs to be as regular as possible to give him time to heal."

Morgan barely heard her. He stared at the man in the bed and let her do her job. Once she left, he moved closer.

"Richard Smalley? Did you grow up on a farm outside Enola?" Even before Richard spoke, Morgan knew the answer.

"Yes." Richard lifted his head of sandy-blond hair, the color of perfectly ripe corn. Morgan knew that color so well, even after all these years.

"It's Morgan, Morgan Ayers. We were friends when we were growing up." He continued staring at the man Richie had become. "What were we, thirteen the last time we saw each other?"

"Yeah. After seventh grade when your dad moved the two of you away. Where did you go? I went away to summer camp, and when I came back you'd moved."

Morgan nodded. "Dad lost his job and got a new one in Detroit, so he packed us up and we moved. Not that we stayed there for very long either. After that we were in Cleveland, and then Pittsburgh, where Dad finally stopped drinking and we could settle down. He remarried, and that's where I spent my last few years of high school." God, he wanted to hurry forward and give Richard a hug, but he didn't have the right any longer. It had been decades, but Morgan had never forgotten Richie. How could he? "I wrote you, but I was thirteen and...."

"Yeah. It wasn't like there was Facebook back then."

Richard was definitely happier than he'd been, with a hint of the smile Morgan remembered from his friend. The memories had dulled over time as the years had gone by, but Morgan would never forget Richie, no matter how long he lived. That wasn't possible. How did you forget the one person you told your deepest, darkest secrets to, and he'd not only understood but told you his in return? How did you forget the boy who had made things better and brought you home when your dad drank most of the grocery money away? Richie had been the one who'd helped see that he didn't starve more times than he wanted to remember.

"You're a firefighter?" Richie asked. "You always said that was what you wanted to be when you grew up, even back then."

"Yeah, and it's a good thing I was, because I hauled you out of the bedroom last night."

"I thought I was dead. I got so disoriented I thought the bedroom door was the way out, and then after that I didn't have the lung power to do anything else. The door closed, and that's the last thing I remember."

"I broke it down and got you out of there, carried you out over my shoulder." He pulled the chair closer to the bed, moved his jacket, and sat down. "You were out of it, but I got you out in time, and once they get the smoke out, you should be good to go."

Richie yanked the covers to the side. "I'll never be good to go again, Morgan." He looked down at his legs. "The best I can do is wheel myself around, but I'm assuming my chair got fried."

"Along with everything else, I'm afraid. The fire was really hot, and I got you out just before it broke through. Damn thing chased me to the door." He wished he had better news.

"Did everyone else get out?" Richie asked.

"Yeah. They were pretty shaken up, and the Red Cross was helping them. But they were all okay."

"I served with Grace's brother in Iraq," Richie said.

"You always wanted to be a soldier," Morgan said. "Marine?"

"Yeah."

Richie looked totally pained, and he had to be wearing out. There were so many questions Morgan wanted to ask, but Richie was fading, and wearing him out wasn't going to do any good.

"I think I'm getting tired."

Morgan nodded and was about to stand up.

"You aren't going to disappear for a few decades again, are you?" Richie asked.

"No. I'm going to head home to get some rest since I just got off shift, but I'll stop by later today to make sure you're doing okay, and we can talk some more." Morgan stood and found a pen and pad on the tray. He jotted down his number for Richie. "I'll see you later."

They shared a smile, and then Richie's eyes drifted closed, so Morgan left the room.

He walked back through the hospital hallways in a slight daze, unable to believe he'd found his friend after all these years. By the time he made it to the exit, he was grinning like an idiot, and his spirit felt lighter than it had in a very long time. He had no logical reason to feel that way. But it didn't seem to matter.

He drove home humming to himself. He was fucking *humming*. Morgan rarely hummed, sang, or whistled. He turned on the radio, and within moments he was singing along with the music. By the time he got home, Morgan was damn near giddy. And he was never that happy or excited about much of anything. God, he was so pathetic. He worked, took care of his home, worked some more, and slept. That was his life, and it had been that way for so long he couldn't remember anything different.

Since he was a municipal employee of Harrisburg, he was required to live in the city. Luckily years ago he'd been able to buy a house in the Italian Lake neighborhood. It was one of the nicer areas of the city. He pulled his car into the garage and hoisted his bag of gear out of the trunk before heading inside.

Morgan dropped his gear in the foyer and continued on through the house, where he checked the mail and took a few minutes to answer some e-mails before heading to the bathroom.

A shower, comfortable clothes, and a light blanket later, he was curled on the sofa, watching television and trying to relax. But all he kept thinking of was Richie and wondering what he'd been through. To say that Richie had been through a lot had to be an understatement. He knew there was something traumatic behind his inability to walk, but there was more than that. His reaction told Morgan that Richie didn't think he had much to live for, and that was really sad, because the Richie he remembered was pretty damned special.

ANDREW GREY is the author of more than one hundred works of Contemporary Gay Romantic fiction. After twenty-seven years in corporate America, he has now settled down in Central Pennsylvania with his husband of more than twenty-five years, Dominic, and his laptop. An interesting ménage. Andrew grew up in western Michigan with a father who loved to tell stories and a mother who loved to read them. Since then he has lived throughout the country and traveled throughout the world. He is a recipient of the RWA Centennial Award, has a master's degree from the University of Wisconsin–Milwaukee, and now writes full-time. Andrew's hobbies include collecting antiques, gardening, and leaving his dirty dishes anywhere but in the sink (particularly when writing). He considers himself blessed with an accepting family, fantastic friends, and the world's most supportive and loving partner. Andrew currently lives in beautiful, historic Carlisle, Pennsylvania.

Email: andrewgrey@comcast.net

Website: www.andrewgreybooks.com

Follow me on BookBub

FIRE AND SAND

ANDREW GREY

A Carlisle Troopers Novel

Can a single dad with a criminal past find love with the cop who pulled him over?

When single dad Quinton Jackson gets stopped for speeding, he thinks he's lost both his freedom and his infant son, who's in the car he's been chasing down the highway. Amazingly, State Trooper Wyatt Nelson not only believes him, he radios for help and reunites Quinton with baby Callum.

Wyatt should ticket Quinton, but something makes him look past Quinton's record. Watching him with his child proves he made the right decision. Quinton is a loving, devoted father—and he's handsome. Wyatt can't help but take a personal interest.

For Quinton, getting temporary custody is a dream come true… or it would be, if working full-time and caring for an infant left time to sleep. As if that weren't enough, Callum's mother will do anything to get him back, including ruining Quinton's life. Fortunately, Quinton has Wyatt for help, support, and as much romance as a single parent can schedule.

But when Wyatt's duties as a cop conflict with Quinton's quest for permanent custody, their situation becomes precarious. Can they trust each other, and the courts, to deliver justice and a happy ever after?

www.dreamspinnerpress.com

TAMING THE
BEAST

ANDREW GREY

"... flat-out wonderful."
-Kate Douglas, author
of the Wolf Tales

A Tale from St. Giles

The suspicious death of Dante Bartholomew's wife changed him, especially in the eyes of the residents of St. Giles. They no longer see a successful businessman… only a monster they believe was involved. Dante's horrific reputation eclipses the truth to the point that he sees no choice but to isolate himself and his heart.

The plan backfires when he meets counselor Beau Clarity and the children he works with. Beau and the kids see beyond the beastly reputation to the beautiful soul inside Dante, and Dante's cold heart begins to thaw as they slip past his defenses. The warmth and hope Beau brings to Dante's life help him see his entire existence—his trials and sorrows—in a brighter light.

But Dante's secrets could rip happiness from their grasp… especially since someone isn't above hurting those Dante has grown to love in order to bring him down.

www.dreamspinnerpress.com

FIRE AND FLINT
ANDREW GREY

CARLISLE
DEPUTIES
1

A Carlisle Deputies Novel

Jordan Erichsohn suspects something is rotten about his boss, Judge Crawford. Unfortunately he has nowhere to turn and doubts anyone will believe his claims—least of all the handsome deputy, Pierre Ravelle, who has been assigned to protect the judge after he received threatening letters. The judge has a long reach, and if he finds out Jordan's turned on him, he might impede Jordan adopting his son, Jeremiah.

When Jordan can no longer stay silent, he gathers his courage and tells Pierre what he knows. To his surprise and relief, Pierre believes him, and Jordan finds an ally… and maybe more. Pierre vows to do what it takes to protect Jordan and Jeremiah and see justice done. He's willing to fight for the man he's growing to love and the family he's starting to think of as his own. But Crawford is a powerful and dangerous enemy, and he's not above ripping apart everything Jordan and Pierre are trying to build in order to save himself….

www.dreamspinnerpress.com

REKINDLED FLAME

ANDREW GREY

Rekindled Flame: Book One

Firefighter Morgan has worked hard to build a home for himself after a nomadic childhood. When Morgan is called to a fire, he finds the family out front, but their tenant still inside. He rescues Richard Smalley, who turns out to be an old friend he hasn't seen in years and the one person he regretted leaving behind.

Richard has had a hard life. He served in the military, where he lost the use of his legs, and has been struggling to make his way since coming home. Now that he no longer has a place to live, Morgan takes him in, but when someone attempts to set fire to Morgan's house, they both become suspicious and wonder what's going on.

Years ago Morgan was gutted when he moved away, leaving Richard behind, so he's happy to pick things up where they left off. But now that Richard seems to be the target of an arsonist, he may not be the safest person to be around.

www.dreamspinnerpress.com

FIRE AND WATER

ANDREW GREY

CARLISLE COPS
1

Carlisle Cops: Book One

Officer Red Markham knows about the ugly side of life after a car accident left him scarred and his parents dead. His job policing the streets of Carlisle, PA, only adds to the ugliness, and lately, drug overdoses have been on the rise. One afternoon, Red is dispatched to the local Y for a drowning accident involving a child. Arriving on site, he finds the boy rescued by lifeguard Terry Baumgartner. Of course, Red isn't surprised when gorgeous Terry won't give him and his ugly mug the time of day.

Overhearing one of the officer's comments about him being shallow opens Terry's eyes. Maybe he isn't as kindhearted as he always thought. His friend Julie suggests he help those less fortunate by delivering food to the elderly. On his route he meets outspoken Margie, a woman who says what's on her mind. Turns out, she's Officer Red's aunt.

Red and Terry's worlds collide as Red tries to track the source of the drugs and protect Terry from an ex-boyfriend who won't take no for an answer. Together they might discover a chance for more than they expected—if they can see beyond what's on the surface.

www.dreamspinnerpress.com